The
Castle in the
Sea

Also by Scott O'Dell

The Black Pearl
The Captive
Carlota
Child of Fire
The Cruise of the Arctic Star
The Dark Canoe
The Feathered Serpent
The Hawk That Dare Not Hunt by Day
Island of the Blue Dolphins
Journey to Jericho
Kathleen, Please Come Home
The King's Fifth
Sarah Bishop
Sing Down the Moon
The Spanish Smile
The 290
Zia
The Amethyst Ring

The
Castle in the
Sea

SCOTT O'DELL

Houghton Mifflin Company   Boston   1983

Library of Congress Cataloging in Publication Data

O'Dell, Scott.
  The castle in the sea.

  Summary: The inheritance of her father's vast
fortune and contact with a variety of people with sus-
picious motives trigger a series of attempts on
Lucinda's life in her isolated island home, which is a
stronghold of Spain within the boundaries of the
United States.
  I. Title.
PZ7.0237Cas   1983   [Fic]   83-12870
ISBN 0-395-34831-5

Printed in the United States of America

Q   10 9 8 7 6 5 4 3 2 1

My name is Ozymandias, king of kings:
Look on my works, ye Mighty, and despair!
— PERCY BYSSHE SHELLEY

Contents

1.

The Snakeskin Case

ON THAT MORNING I RESCUED THE PORTRAIT OF Teresa de Cabrillo y Benivides from the dusty hell-hole where it had sat for months and hung it again on the wall in the music room.

I had stood before this portrait of my ancestress, admiring her eyes, which were the color of mist as the sun rises, of silver when it comes pure from the furnace, tinged with the faintest hint of blue; admiring most of all her smile, which once had seemed bereft, about to speak some sad warning, but now said to me, "This life is mine, Lucinda, not yours. Go and live your own life. And whatever you find there, smile as I am smiling now."

Afterwards, I sent for Ricardo Villaverde, who had been my father's servant and loyal friend. When nearly an hour passed and Señor Villaverde didn't appear, I went to his quarters. Once my father's, they overlooked our chapel and were reached by climbing a long flight of spiral stairs. The door was ajar. Receiving no answer to my knock, I walked in.

The two staghounds my father had owned rose from a corner and came forward to confront me, their eyes aglow. After sniffing my shoes they backed away and disappeared, growling as they went.

I had not been in my father's rooms for more than a year, not since the time when he lay ill and I had gone to visit him. Nothing had changed. The stark white walls were bare except for a crucifix. The wooden floor was without covering. The narrow bed, reached by three steps, was in the same position — set in such a way that my father, before he closed his eyes at night and again when he opened them at dawn, could look down into the chapel at the figure of the Virgin Mary.

There were four large closets in his quarters. In two of them hung the doublets and cloaks he wore when he wished to appear as a nobleman at the court of Ferdinand and Isabella. The third closet held the modern clothes he wore when he went to Spain on business. In the fourth closet he kept walking sticks, umbrellas, and traveling bags, some old, some new, one of them a cloth bag my great-great-great-grandfather had carried when he came to Spanish California in the year 1821.

I chose four of the smallest and newest bags and was about to shut the closet door when I heard steps behind me and caught the faint scent of a cologne my father sometimes used. I turned to see Villaverde crossing the room, walking softly on his rubber heels, a startled expression on his face. He recognized me at once and threw up his hands in mock surprise.

"Sorry, Señorita Lucinda," he said, showily rolling his *r*'s. "For a moment I thought you were Alicia, who of late spends most of her time nosing about."

He glanced at the suitcases piled up beside the closet door and frowned. Then he smiled to hide his displeasure.

"You are borrowing the suitcases for someone?" he asked. "Someone is going to the mainland?"

"Yes," I said. "Will you see that they are taken to the tower?"

"I will take them myself," he said, picking up two of the suitcases. "Which tower, Señorita Lucinda?"

"The south tower," I said. "Mine."

Villaverde set the suitcases carefully on the floor and began to wipe them off with a cloth he took from his pocket. As I left the room he came running after me, leaving the suitcases behind.

"It is you," he said, staring at me. "It is you who's going."

"Tomorrow," I said, though it was none of his business. "If the weather stays good."

He fumbled with the cleaning cloth, shook it out, and folded it up into a billy club. He struck himself with it, a sharp blow on the thigh. He was trying hard to conceal his anger.

"Your father will not approve of this journey," he told me.

"Don Enrique is dead," I reminded him.

"But before he died, he gave me certain responsibilities. On my knees I swore a solemn oath to discharge them. The chief of these is to see that you do not leave this island. Not until you reach the age of eighteen and can decide for yourself, not as a headstrong girl, but as a mature, sensible woman."

"You have no authority over what I do. You are not my guardian."

I started to leave the chapel. He reached out and grasped my arm.

Villaverde was short and thin, but heavy lifts in his shoes gave him a look of height. He wore a black wig, luxuriant and curled. Underneath — I had seen it only once, as a frightened child — was a white, oblong skull with a ridge running down the middle.

I had never liked Villaverde. Since the days of my childhood he had made me uncomfortable. I disliked his habit of wandering through the castle — you would meet him in the most unexpected places day or night — and returning to my father to report whatever he found amiss, be it smoking candles or a small theft of food or something more important, like a rude remark he had overheard about the master of Isla del Oro.

In time I had come to hate Villaverde, not in his role as mayordomo, but for encouraging my father over the years in the mad scheme that had filled his crypt with eighteen coffins — Margaret Drew of the rosebud mouth, the first young woman to come to Isla del Oro; Helen Barnes, who looked like a Raphael madonna; Linda, the girl who wrote romantic poetry; Kimberley Wood, of the golden hair; and all the others — dead, all dead and hidden in their crystal caskets in my father's marble crypt.

There was no evidence to prove that Villaverde had been an accomplice in this ghastly affair. The courts had absolved him of any complicity. Yet I knew he was guilty of these crimes — as guilty as my father, Don Enrique de Cabrillo y Benivides. And Villaverde was well aware that I knew it. He also knew that I was only waiting for an excuse to banish him from Isla del Oro.

But was it an excuse I waited for? Was it not something far stronger that held me back? Was it that now, at this very moment, as we confronted each other in the dim anteroom, I heard not him but my father speaking? It was Don Enrique's same Andalusian accent. His habit of pausing between words, ending a sentence with a rising inflection. The arrogance behind the soft words. Villaverde's hatred of the *gringo* — the outlaws and adventurers who had seized California from Spain and robbed her of the whole Southwest — was as violent as my father's. More so.

He studied me, one eye half-closed, trying to gauge how far he dared go. Suddenly he smiled, a friendly show of white teeth, each as perfect as a pearl, and released my arm.

"Hola," he said softly, "let's not quarrel. It will not please your father." He spoke of Don Enrique as if he were still alive, sitting at that moment in the library, reading Plutarch and smoking one of his pale cigars.

"But you'll return soon enough," he said. "It won't take you long to get your fill of the barbarians."

5

He returned upstairs for two of the bags and brought them down, calling back that he would bring the others in a short time, trying to leave the impression that he welcomed my journey. And yet I could be wrong. Possibly he really was glad to have me leave the island. His objection to my leaving could be a ruse, disguising a wish to undertake some dubious scheme as soon as my back was turned.

I picked up the bags, deciding to carry them myself, when I recalled that my father had owned a black attaché case that he used on the trips he made to Spain. Fashioned in Madrid of the finest snakeskin, equipped with gold clasps and two gold locks, each with three secret numbers to dial, and fitted with numerous pockets — one for toilet articles, one for gold pens, one, carefully sealed, to keep cigars fresh, one for paper and writing pads, and even a small compartment with its own secret lock — the black snakeskin case had always intrigued me. I climbed the stairs again to look for it.

Rummaging in the closet, just as I was about to give up the search, I came upon it. I took it down and started for the tower, stopping only in the chapel to thank the Blessed Virgin for my good fortune and to ask her guidance on my journey.

The other big bags were lying on my bed when I got there. Waiting for me were Father Martínez, smiling broadly; my friend and servant, Mercedes Ochoa, with a long face and a bottle of smelling salts; silent Alicia; and Villaverde himself, rubbing his thin wrists, eager to see that everything went well.

Mercedes said, "I wish you had some new bags. I saw beautiful ones in the newspaper. Some small, some large, and in all colors. Pink would be good. I like the red ones, too."

A Los Angeles newspaper was delivered to the island on Sundays, the editions so big they had to be tied together with wire. None of the servants could read, but all of them loved the pictures, especially the ads for clothes and cosmetics. They spent the morning looking at the paper and did no work. Once I took the occasion to give them a stern lecture, which brought lamentations and tears. They would be glad to be rid of me, no doubt, if only for a month or so.

The thought was not unsettling. I would be equally glad to get rid of all thirty-one of them — and their gossipy meetings, during which they drank gallons of chocolate beaten to a froth. As soon as I returned to the island I would give thought to dismissing a dozen of them.

Not a difficult task. Don Enrique had insisted that every room in Castillo Santiago be ready for guests at all times — both drawing rooms, both refectories, all three breakfast rooms (including the terrace where lanterns hung and wind bells tinkled in summer), and each of the thirty bedrooms, the bed covers turned down, Swiss chocolates on the pillows, fresh flowers in the golden vases. No matter that few guests ever came or were invited. I would put an end to this prideful extravagance and run the castle with half the number of servants who now gossiped and drank chocolate and complained.

"With your permission," Mercedes said, "I will order some new suitcases for you. Two pink, two red. They will be here in three days, maybe."

"In three days I'll be gone, flying high over the United States of America. Far away from you, thank heavens."

Grumbling, consoling herself with the bottle of smelling salts, with Alicia's help Mercedes packed the four bags with clothes I had already laid out. When she came to the attaché case she fumbled at the locks, then turned to me in desperation.

I thought hard. For ten minutes or more I tried to remember the combination and failed. I tried various combinations, starting with the number 1 on each of the dials.

"Mathematically speaking," Father Martínez said with some impatience, "there are nine hundred and ninety-nine thousand, nine hundred and ninety-nine combinations on the locks. You could be here until tomorrow trying to find the right ones."

Villaverde was silent, watching me from across the room, still chafing his thin wrists, one eye half-closed, as customary.

I concentrated again. I had a good memory. I could read a page in a book and then repeat it word for word. The combination would surely have some personal meaning to my father. And what could be more personal than his birthday, the day Don Enrique de Cabrillo y Benivides came into the world?

He was born on May 23 in the year 1932. These numbers would not fit the dials, but the date 23 and the number 5, for the fifth month on the calendar, would. I tried 235 with each of the dials. The case snapped open with a hollow thud. Pandora, the first woman ever created by Vulcan, god of fire, must have heard the same sound, opening the box in which Prometheus had confined all the evils that could trouble mankind.

I raised the lid to reveal a scroll tied with a ribbon and sealed with wax. It was very similar in appearance to the will in which my father had named me as his heiress, the will he angrily had thrown in the fire. Could it be the testament that my lawyer, Don Anselmo, and I had scoured the library and unsuccessfully rifled every safe in the castle trying to find?

The wax seal was marked with Don Enrique's thumbprint. The fancy red ribbon was tied in a bowknot, but backwards — so that the knot had a habit of slanting off to one side instead of remaining straight. The scroll itself was the heavy gray parchment with gold edges that he used in all of his personal correspondence.

My first impulse was to leave the scroll where it was; to lock the case and have Mercedes put it away. For some reason — could it be that at this moment an urgent hand reached out and touched mine? — I picked up the scroll. But trembling as I was, it fell from my grasp. Before I could move, Villaverde slipped across the room without a sound. Gathering up the scroll, he handed it to me with a quick, obsequious servant's smile and bow. He bowed again as he backed across the room.

Father Martínez said, "Read it, Lucinda. It may be the testament you have searched for and never found."

Against my will, led by the same strange hand whose touch I had felt before, I broke the seal and untied the ribbon. At a glance I saw that the writing was in my father's curious hand and signed with his elaborate signature of a dozen loops and flourishes set down in one grand sweep without taking pen from paper. Once more I was seized by the impulse to hide the scroll, never to see it. To have it destroyed, given to the flames.

"Here," Father Martínez said, seeing my distress, "give it to me. I'll not make it out as well as you could. If I get into trouble, you'll help me out."

I didn't answer. He took it from my hand and walked to the wall mirror. Don Enrique had used his curious script in the testament, in which the sentences read from right to left with the words upside down so that they had to be read in a mirror. Father Martínez began to read in a halting voice, stumbling over the first sentence. With a shrug of apology, Father Martínez turned to me for help.

I walked to the window and looked out at the sky of driving clouds and the yellow waves breaking on the headland. He went on as best he could, without me, stumbling along after numerous pauses and corrections.

The document was Don Enrique's last will and testament, drawn up and dated a week before his death. It left all of his properties to his daughter, Lucinda de

Cabrillo y Benivides — the island of Isla del Oro, oil-fields in Venezuela, a copper mine in Peru, leagues of the Mexican coast planted to pineapples and known as the Blue Beach, on and on, a long list.

Near the end of the testament Father Martínez came to a halt. He read the word *because,* changed it to *be it known,* and halted again. As I turned around he crossed himself. His jaws suddenly tightened and he grew pale.

"Stop," I cautioned him. "It's not necessary to read more. We know the rest. It's exactly like the testament he burned."

"A good idea," Father Martínez said, handing me the testament. "It's long-winded. Do as you wish, but I suggest you put it in the safe."

"Don Enrique writes so beautifully," Villaverde said in his soft voice, "with such elegance, such command of the priceless Andalusian tongue, I would like to hear more. That is, *señorita,* if it doesn't disturb you to hear your father speak again."

I glanced at him, standing with his thin hands neatly folded, and said, to let him know that I was not affected in any way, and that if I were it was none of his concern, "It doesn't disturb me in the least. Why should it?"

Villaverde bowed and muttered an apology, but I thought I saw a cold glint in his eye. Finding the place where Father Martínez had halted, I read on.

"Be it known, because of his lifelong devotion to the causes of our dear mother, the glorious kingdom of Iberia, famed since the days of Rome, because of

11

his loyalty to me likewise, in all times and all weathers of the soul, I wish and declare that my dear friend and companion, Ricardo Villaverde, shall be herewith and until the day of her maturity, my daughter's adviser and watchful guardian . . ."

There was more to the testament, but before I could read on, Villaverde slipped across the room and in one swift moment, no longer the soft-spoken servant, the obedient, fawning retainer, snatched the parchment from my hand. At the door he turned to face me.

"I advise you to unpack your bags," he said.

"Why?" I answered.

"Because you are not leaving the island."

I stared at him, not sure of what I had heard.

"You are not leaving the island," he said again. "Is that clear?"

I took a step toward him and stopped. "It's clear, *señor,* very clear. And may I make it clear to you that I intend to leave the island. Tomorrow."

"Not tomorrow, nor the day after tomorrow," he said.

Father Martínez came and stood beside me. "You are speaking as a guardian, which you are not, *señor,* not yet, not until the day the will is delivered to the courts and probated."

"Courts dither and dally for weeks, often for months," Villaverde said, waving the testament in our faces. "In the meantime, here in my hand, placed in my keeping, are the expressed hopes and desires of Don Enrique de Cabrillo y Benivides. I have been charged by him with a solemn duty. I intend, though it should mean my life, to see that this duty is discharged."

He put the testament in his pocket and closed the door behind him. I heard his footsteps hurrying down the marble stairs.

2.

The Steel Bracelet

WITHIN AN HOUR, ALTHOUGH A STORM THREATENED to descend upon us, Señor Villaverde was on his way to the mainland aboard the *Infanta*. We learned from the captain when the ship returned three days later that he had taken a plane for Seville. Why he had gone to Spain and how long he planned to remain there, Captain Orozco couldn't say, nor would he hazard a guess.

At noon I was driven to the harbor and put aboard the *Infanta* with my four big bags and the black snakeskin case. A crowd of miners' wives were at the wharf to send me off, and marimbas piped me up the gangplank with a lively tune. But upon reaching the deck I was confronted by Captain Orozco.

I hadn't seen him since the night he took the place of Captain Wolfe, an hour after Wolfe's death. During the few times he had eaten dinner in the castle, I had come to dislike Orozco. It might have been the fancy bracelets he wore on his hairy wrists, or the way he had of glancing at himself in all the mirrors he passed, or just the silly notion I got that his large crooked nose made him look like an aging bird of prey. He was embarrassed. He tried to smile. Taking off his gold-encrusted cap, he put it on again. He glanced at the radar churning around overhead and the dark sky beyond, streaked with driving clouds.

"It's not a good time to make crossings," he said. "In a day or two the storm will remove itself. I suggest that you wait until it does."

"I wish to leave now," I said.

"The channel's very rough, Miss Lucinda."

"I am used to rough seas," I said. "I've seen them all my life."

"They're rougher than any in years. I've just come in . . ."

"I know you have. You took Señor Villaverde to the mainland and the last thing he said to you when he left the ship was, 'Captain Orozco, do not under any circumstances permit the girl to leave the island.' And then he showed you my father's will. Then he pretended to read it to you, the part where it speaks of Villaverde as my guardian."

Captain Orozco wore a small beard on his chin, pointed and curled at the ends. It moved now, ever so slightly — the only sign that my words had surprised him.

"Señor Villaverde," I said, "is not my guardian until the day the will is probated. At this moment I am under the protection of my lawyer, Don Anselmo de Alicantera. I can visit the mainland, if I wish. And storm or no storm, whatever Señor Villaverde has said, I wish to do so."

From under the brim of his gold-braided cap, Orozco studied me for a moment, weighing future possibilities. If he chose to follow Villaverde's command, to defy my wishes, he would lose his job the day I came of age. If he didn't obey Villaverde's command, he would lose his job the day the *señor* was made my guardian. It was a difficult choice.

He squared his shoulders and stepped out from under the awning to take a look at the sky. Then he excused himself, went to the bridge, and came back with a weather report.

"According to the Coast Guard," he said, "we're in for hard winds. The eye of the storm lies north-northwest of San Pedro de Mártir in central Baja, headed in our direction at sixty knots. It will hit the channel in an hour or less."

I was certain that Captain Orozco was telling the truth. The storm had been building up for days. At this moment shredded clouds were streaming in from Mexico and rain had begun to fall, fat drops that spattered on the deck. But I had thought about this journey for years. I had dreamed about it. I had looked forward to the day when I could cross the channel and see for myself what lay in the mysterious land that my father loved, whose *gringo* inhabitants he reviled.

"Do we have a worthy ship?" I said. Captain Orozco nodded. "Then let us go."

16

Orozco saluted stiffly and climbed the ladder to the ship's bridge. I followed him. The big diesels turned over and settled down to a steady purr. The hawsers came in. As the ship edged away from the wharf, miners shot off charges of dynamite and the marimba band played "El Rancho Grande."

A heavy gust of wind struck our bow as we headed for the Narrows. The two promontories that formed this passage and protected the harbor from the sea were hidden in spray. From far off I heard the sound of a whistling buoy.

A ray of sun broke through the overcast. It shone for an instant upon the four towers of Castillo Santiago, turning the copper plates that sheathed them into smoldering fires. I saw the window, small and barred like a window in a prison, through which I had often gazed at the sea and the distant shores of California.

We were now close upon the headlands, barely visible through the driving spray, that formed the narrow passage to the sea. Orozco bent forward to adjust the knob on the radar, and as he did so the light from the screen turned his hand a greenish yellow. It looked like the hand of a man long dead, like my father's hand.

The bracelet on the captain's wrist turned the same strange color. Suddenly there was a bracelet on my own wrist, the bracelet with links of unyielding steel that Don Enrique once had placed there. I was a child again. I was on the way to visit my ancient grandmother, Doña Gertrudis, guarded by two Yaqui *pisto-*

17

leros, chained to my Indian nurse so that I would not be tempted to stray, so the barbarians would not harm me.

The chain seemed real. It bit into my flesh. Then I felt a hand on my shoulder, holding me. A voice said ever so softly in my ear, "Turn back, Lucinda. Turn back."

I must have made a sound or uttered some frightened word, for Captain Orozco glanced at me in alarm. "You're deathly pale. Are you sick?" he asked.

"Turn back," I said through trembling lips.

Miners set off dynamite squibs that swished through the pelting rain. Women fell to their knees and tearfully thanked God. The marimbas played "El Rancho Grande" again. Everyone was overjoyed that I had been saved by the wisdom of Captain Orozco, who had wisely turned back at the very mouth of the Narrows, just as the hurricane was about to engulf us. I said nothing to make them think otherwise.

Father Martínez suggested that we all thank the Queen of Heaven for Her intercession in my behalf. We could have thanked Her there on the wharf, but he insisted that this would be unseemly. Instead, he led the way up the winding road, in the wind and pummeling rain, to the doors of the chapel. He stood aside to let us pass, then closed the doors and talked for a long time. I heard only a few words of what he said and remembered nothing.

Shivering, I still felt the steel bracelet on my wrist and heard the words whispered softly in my ear. Was my father to rule me even in death, as he had in life?

18

Would visions of him continue to haunt me through all my days?

I didn't wait for confession — I had nothing to confess except fear. As I went quickly down the aisle, I glanced up at the little window and the screen that shielded my father's bedroom, where he could lie in bed like his hero, King Philip, and feast his eyes on the Madonna.

He was not behind the screen or the little window with its leaded panes. I didn't expect to see him, yet I glanced up a second time, searching for his tormented face. With relief I saw that he was not there. In his place I saw the muzzles of the two great staghounds pressing against the glass, their amber eyes fixed upon me.

3.

The Telegram

I FLED TO THE TOWER AND BOLTED THE DOOR BEHIND me, furious at myself.

For months I had dreamed of the journey to the mainland, how exciting it would be after my years as a prisoner to see new places again, above all to meet new people, even if they proved to be what my father had told me they were — a race of greedy barbarians. And yet, her clothes packed and everything attended to, standing on the ship's bridge, headed for the open sea and the mainland, Lucinda de Cabrillo y Benivides had given up her dream.

I went to the window and flung open the heavy shutters. The white hull of the *Infanta* barely showed through the mist. The sky was gray and still and the sea beyond seemed just another part of the gray sky.

An hour must have passed while I stood at the window — one moment a featherless fledgling who didn't know her own mind; the next moment, a cringing coward. Then I was grown up, resolute, making plans to start on the journey as soon as the storm abated. But at last, as a knock came at the door, I was again the slave, hearing my father's whispered words, feeling the steel bracelet upon my wrist.

When I didn't answer, a second knock followed, and a third. The oak door was six inches thick, iron-banded, and fastened with two heavy bolts. "You were not at vespers," Father Martínez said from behind it. "I missed you."

"You haven't come to lecture me," I warned him through the door.

"Only a word or two of a friendly nature," he said softly. "You are blaming yourself for something that's not your fault. I wish to lighten your burden."

He sounded like a mendicant standing out in the cold, begging for alms. But once I let him in and he had hitched up his gown, his tone quickly changed.

"For whatever reason, you've decided to postpone the journey. You should —"

"It's not postponed," I said. "I've given up all thought of going. I plan to live every day of the rest of my life on Isla del Oro."

"There are worse fates," he observed under his breath. Then, speaking boldly, he said, "You will go someday when you're better prepared for the rigors of the undertaking."

I challenged him. "In other words, when I have grown up?"

"In other words, no. You could grow up and live your whole life and still be in thrall. You'll be prepared for the journey when you realize that your father is dead. Not here to hold your hand in love and the next moment to chastise you for some fancied misdeed. When you no longer hear a ghostly voice threatening you."

"Who told you that I hear ghostly voices?" I said. "That I am in thrall to an unhappy past?"

"No one," Father Martínez said, planting his feet more firmly, the better to withstand what might come. "I saw it when you were reading Don Enrique's will. Your voice trembled. You turned pale unto death. Every other second you glanced at his bags lying on the bed, as if you expected to see him appear at any moment, toss your clothes on the floor, close the bags, and take them away."

I said nothing in reply, for this was the truth. I had seen my father standing by the bed, listening to me read his will, while I stuttered, losing my voice completely when I came to the words *Ricardo Villaverde shall be herewith and until the day of her maturity my daughter's adviser and watchful guardian.*

"The same grim specter stood beside you on the ship the moment you ordered Captain Orozco to turn back."

Once more, as I faced Father Martínez, I felt the chain fasten upon my wrist. I glanced down, expecting to find it there.

"Now that you have given up the journey and decided to live the rest of your life on Isla del Oro, it would be well if you assumed some of your responsibilities. Not sit idly by and let Captain Vega and his *pistoleros* run wild. For instance, there's the problem of the news reporter."

A man from one of the Los Angeles newspapers had suddenly appeared at the gate of the castle. He had been turned away, but eluded the *pistoleros* and was now holed up in one of the mines.

"Vega wants to blast him out," Father Martínez went on. "It would be better if you took a hand and decided on a more humane way to get rid of him. Another problem, the *penitentes*. The Indian cult is no longer satisfied to parade at Easter with their cross and bleeding Christ, but now are parading each Sunday, scoffing at the church. Furthermore, now that half the world seems to be watching us, we should keep a tight rein on Captain Vega."

Sightseers in droves were still cruising up and down the shore, snapping pictures of the castle where horrible crimes had taken place, hoping to catch a glimpse of the strange, beautiful girl who owned the island, who, according to the newspapers, lived alone under the baleful eye of an eccentric priest, guarded by a hundred armed *vaqueros,* waited upon by dozens of wild, barefooted Indians and black-browed servants from Spain.

Father Martínez, warming to his task, decided to sit. "Since Don Enrique's death," he said, "since he abandoned his crazy idea of capturing the atomic plant at San Onofre, Vega hasn't had anything to do except to keep sightseers off the island. We must think of something more adventurous. He's a restless spirit. He can be dangerous in some unheard-of way. Right now he's bothering the Coast Guard and the lighthouse they're trying to finish at Punta del Sur. Your father fought them for years and Vega's carrying on the fight, with Villaverde's help. We need to stop this and let the Coast Guard get on with their job."

The wind was screaming now, filling the room with strange echoes that distorted his words. The village and the bay and the sea had disappeared. The world outside was a curtain of cold, gray mist, streaming endlessly past the window.

Father Martínez said, "You also are neglecting your mail. It's piling up downstairs. You haven't even bothered to have it brought here to the tower."

The last letters I had written were in answer to a graduate student in agronomy, who was looking for a place to grow his special variety of *Agaricus campestris.* And a reply to one from a man who said, "I am a blue-eyed sailor, aged one half-century, seeking a snug harbor with a supportive, vibrant woman, who you seem to be judging from your picture in the newspaper."

Father Martínez had more to say about things I should and shouldn't do, the last being a warning about the serpent that had killed my father.

"It's still wandering about down there in the crypt," he said. "You should have it rounded up and destroyed before it kills someone else."

I could think of no reply, so I wished him good night and went to bed. In less than a minute there came another knock at the door, and Mercedes burst in, out of breath, and handed me a message delivered by wireless from Los Angeles to the *Infanta*.

It was from Doña Octavia de Puertoblanco, the mother of my fiancé, Porfirio de Puertoblanco. Sent from New York, it read, "Don Porfirio and I arrive tomorrow morning in Los Angeles. Can you make arrangements to meet us?"

There was more, but I didn't read on. I was overcome with a sudden faintness. I sat down in the nearest chair and stared at Mercedes, who stared back at me.

"Your *novio*," she said, still breathless, not sure whether to laugh or cry. Neither was I. "And you've never set eyes on him. How exciting! But he's not a real stranger. You've written letters."

"Not many. One month ago, telling him about Don Enrique. But before that, not more than two or three altogether."

"But you have many pictures of him. I saw them before you put them away."

I got up and dug a big one in a silver frame out of the bureau drawer where I had put it months before, while Christopher Dawson was still on the island. Porfirio hadn't changed. He still looked out at me with an arrogant sidelong glance, his sideburns too long and curly, his nose sniffing the air like an aristocratic hound.

"He's wonderfully handsome," Mercedes said. "How happy you'll be! And you deserve it ... it's been a long, long engagement."

"Three years. Since I was thirteen years and five months."

"It's too bad Don Enrique won't be here to enjoy the wedding. But how lucky you didn't go sailing off today! That would have been terrible — you there and Don Porfirio here, miles apart." She paused for a rapturous sigh. "Do you wish me to start preparations tomorrow? There's much to be done . . . the castle's in terrible shape for a wedding."

"Wait until the Puertoblancos arrive," I said.

That night as I lay in bed wooing sleep, trying to pull myself together, disturbed by several dynamite blasts, a passage from *Vanity Fair* kept running through my thoughts.

"O you poor women!" Thackeray had written. "O you poor secret martyrs and victims, whose life is torture, who are stretched on racks in your bedrooms, and who lay your heads down on the block daily at the drawing-room table; every man who watches your pains, or peers into those dark places where the torture is administered to you, must pity you — and thank God that he has a beard."

In the morning, one of the problems on the long list Father Martínez had presented to keep me happy and occupied was solved. The news reporter hiding in an abandoned mine shaft was flushed out by *pistoleros* after a night of dynamite blasts.

The news came at noon, and I immediately sent word to our *calabozo,* where the man was being held on Captain Vega's orders, to have him brought to the castle. He arrived within the hour, escorted by guards.

Father Martínez and I received him in the Great Hall. I sat in a high-backed, brocaded chair, feeling

26

like Isabella, Queen of Castile, when Christopher Columbus stood before her and pled for money to pay for his voyage to the New World. Like King Ferdinand, Father Martínez sat beside me.

The reporter was young, though old enough to grow a beard that covered most of his face. Since most homely men, I had observed, chose to cover their faces with hair, I judged him to be homely. Father Martínez asked his name.

"Ed Adams," the news reporter said, stuttering a little.

"Why are you here on Isla del Oro?" Father Martínez asked. "Why did you trespass on property that you knew was private?"

"I came to get the truth about the island," Mr. Adams said. "About what has happened here in the past and what may happen in the future. About you, sir. And Lucinda de Cabrillo y Beniventes."

"Benivides," Father Martínez corrected him.

Mr. Adams was clothed in a torn shirt and Levi's that were black with coal dust. On his forehead was a bump, which he kept probing with his finger.

"It seems," he said, "as though I am not on an island in the United States of America, but on an island someplace in Russia."

I spoke up. "You *are* in the United States of America, and the island belongs to me. You are a trespasser, Mr. Adams, an intruder."

"I *must* be in Russia," he insisted, glancing at the guards, who stood on either side of him. "Appearing before some Russian tribunal."

He spoke in Spanish, such bad Spanish that I couldn't understand him. I asked him to try English.

"By what power have you arrested me?" he wanted to know.

"You're not under arrest," Father Martínez replied. "You are simply held as a common nuisance."

Mr. Adams was not discomfited. He fished out a crumpled piece of paper and the stub of a pencil.

"There are a few questions I would like to ask. And since your ship leaves here every week on Fridays, and since I wish to be on it when it sails tomorrow, I'll begin . . ."

"Today is Friday," I interrupted. "You've lost a day somewhere."

"That's better than losing his life," Father Martínez said, "which he was in imminent danger of doing. From his gaunt look he would have starved to death in another week."

"I arrived with rations for a month," Mr. Adams said. "I came prepared for whatever happened."

"Today is Friday, not Thursday," I said, reminding him that his time on Isla del Oro was short. "*Infanta* sails in less than an hour. At two o'clock precisely."

He frowned, tenderly touching the bump on his forehead. "Your father, Don Enrique de Cabrillo y Benivides, died from a snakebite, the bite of a deadly bushmaster. The bushmaster is a native of Central America. How did it ever get on this island, thirty miles from Los Angeles and two thousand miles from its home?"

"A ship carrying a collection of animals and birds

28

bound for the San Francisco zoo ran aground here in a fog and spilled some of her cargo on the beach. Everything was rescued, except a quetzal bird, three rare monkeys, and a pair of bushmasters. The monkeys were found, but only one of the bushmasters. The one that wasn't found killed my father."

"The accident happened where?" Mr. Adams said.

"It was variously reported as taking place in a crypt, in a pantheon, also in one of the mines."

The stubby pencil was poised to take notes.

"I wish you to understand," I said, "that I am talking to you only because I wish to put an end to the rumors and to establish the truth."

"I understand how you feel, Miss Benivides."

"The accident took place in the crypt."

"Can I see this crypt?"

"You *may* not," I said, correcting his English.

"There's a room filled with tombs somewhere in the castle."

"The pantheon. It preserves the remains of Juan Rodriguez Cabrillo, discoverer of this island in the year fifteen forty-two. And those of Gaspar de Portolá, who traveled two thousand leagues from Mexico, across the Vermilion Sea and the vast Desert of Vizcaíno, into a village of ragged savages who ate acorns and stewed lizards, the village that was to become the great city of Los Angeles." Guiltily, though it was really none of his business, I failed to say that Portolá's bones were not his but those of a Nayarit Indian.

Mr. Adams held his piece of paper to the light.

29

"Miss Benivides," he said, without looking away from the paper. "You're reported to be the richest girl in the world. Is this true?"

"I haven't the faintest idea."

"One of the richest?"

"It is possible."

Mr. Adams glanced around the Great Hall, at the glittering chandeliers, at the Gobelin tapestries on the walls; then at me. "Richest or one of the richest, it doesn't matter," he said. "I am curious about the source of your wealth. The miners who produce it. I understand that their wages are shamefully low. Only half of the wages paid on the mainland."

"The miners come from Mexico," Father Martínez said. "In Mexico, if they had a job, which is unlikely, they would earn less than a dollar a day."

"In other words, they're aliens and as aliens, they are exploited."

Mr. Adams was looking at me, not at Father Martínez, trying to get me to answer. I knew nothing about the men, what they were paid. As far as I knew, they and their wives and children were happy.

"Is it true that the miners and their families, once they're here, never leave the island?" the reporter asked, still addressing me.

Father Martínez spoke for me again. "They live on the island and stay on the island as a matter of choice. In Mexico, hundreds, thousands, clamor to come here."

"Then your island has a steady supply of labor."

"Fortunately," said Father Martínez. "For you can't make soup in a basket."

Did Mr. Adams grit his teeth, or was it a sound from the big clock behind him?

"From what I gather here in this room," he said, not giving up, still fixing me with an inquisitive eye, "you think of yourself as a Spaniard, not an American?"

"We are Spaniards," Father Martínez said.

Mr. Adams kept his gaze fixed upon me, waiting for my answer.

"Both," I said.

He made a note with his stubby pencil, then fixed me again with his inquisitive eye. His eyes were dark blue, as far as I could tell, or perhaps an unusual shade of gray.

"In this crypt, which unfortunately I won't see, there are two or three dozen caskets. Caskets made of gold."

"Fewer than that," I said, "and not gold. Crystal."

"Dr. Wolfe testified during her trial that she had discovered an ancient, secret method of embalming. Did you read about it?"

"No."

"Your father hated Americans," Mr. Adams said. "*Gringos.* Do you harbor the same hatred?"

"I've known only a few *gringos.* Some I liked and some I didn't."

"Could you say the same about the Spaniards you have known?"

"Exactly."

"When do you plan to open Isla del Oro to the public? It's a beautiful island. Thousands would enjoy coming here for a visit, for picnics and vacations and honeymoons."

"Nunca," I said. *"Nunca, nunca."*

He frowned to show his displeasure at what he deemed my arrant selfishness. He studied his piece of paper. It held a long list of questions. I stood up and looked at the clock.

"Infanta leaves in less than an hour," I said. "I would like to see a copy of the paper when it comes out."

"It's not for the newspapers," he said. "It's a book. Books take time. Perhaps I'll bring you a copy when it's published."

"Muchas gracias," I said, sorry for a moment that I had criticized his Spanish. Since he was so earnest about everything, I decided not to tell him that a friend, a journalist, was also writing a book about Isla del Oro.

4.

Uninvited Guests

TOWARD MIDNIGHT OF THE FOLLOWING DAY THE
storm came to an end. A fog rolled in and hid the
mainland coast. It crept westward, shrouding the sea,
then the harbor, and at last the castle itself.

An hour passed. I failed to see *Infanta* arrive. The
first I knew that the ship had returned was when
Mercedes appeared at the door to say that my guests
were downstairs. I hurried into my clothes and ran.

They were in the music room, where I kept the
harpsichord and the painting of Teresa de Cabrillo y
Benivides, my dearly loved ancestress. A youth was
seated on the music bench, running his fingers over
the keys and laughing — apparently at the odd
sounds that came tinkling forth. A woman who stood
behind him was holding her hands over her ears.

The woman bounced forward before I could utter a
word and clasped me in her arms. "My darling Lucinda," she whispered and led me to the bench where

33

the young man sat. "This is your *novio,* my son, Porfirio de Puertoblanco."

Settling the starched cuffs of his shirt, still smiling at the odd sounds of the harpsichord, Don Porfirio rose slowly to his feet. He was much taller than the Porfirio I had imagined. And much older, five years older than I, at least, and strikingly handsome in a dour, taciturn way. A patch he wore over his right eye gave his countenance a piratical look, which was heightened when he limped toward me, leaning on a cane.

"Poor Porfirio," his mother said. "The cane and patch and everything. It all happened just before we left Seville. I hope you'll forgive his dreadful appearance. Oh, dear . . ."

"You are prettier than your photographs," Porfirio said, taking my hand in his. "And older."

"At Lucinda's age," Doña Octavia said, "that is a compliment. I remember when I was twelve I prayed to be eighteen and twenty-one when I was eighteen."

She was now, I guessed, nearly fifty — a long-nosed woman with plump cheeks and thin lips that never seemed to move as she spoke. Porfirio's darkly handsome looks did not come from his mother.

He yawned politely behind his hand. His mother apologized for him. "Poor Porfirio," she said. "On top of everything else, he's had a six-hour flight across the Atlantic and a bumpy five hours from New York."

"And two hours of bumpy seas getting here from Los Angeles," Porfirio said, yawning again. "Have you ever thought of building an airfield?"

34

"No," I said, displeased. "Not once."

"A good idea, though. It's rough out there in your so-called Pacific sea. Rougher than the English Channel."

"You're exaggerating," his mother said. "It really wasn't that bad. You got seasick because you were worn out by the long plane trip. Please go to bed, dear. You'll feel better in the morning."

"It *is* morning, Mother."

"Then you'll feel better when you wake up."

"I hope so, Mother."

"Would you like to sleep where you can hear the waves?" I asked Porfirio.

He shuddered. "No, thank you," he said. "Put me in a quiet room, far removed from all groans and grunts of your ocean."

Mercedes led him away to the west tower, the quietest of the four towers, but where, unfortunately, he would have a full view of the smelter and its belching smokestacks when he awakened in the morning.

After kissing her son goodnight, Doña Octavia lingered on. She was a stout woman with trim ankles and a solid shelf of a bosom, so broad that she seemed to have one breast instead of two.

"You must also be tired," she said, "but I do want to talk. I think it is important that you know at once what brings me here on such short notice. Not as an unwelcome guest, I trust, since your father has often begged me to visit Isla del Oro."

"You have always been welcome and you are

welcome now," I said, stretching the truth.

"I have thought of you day and night since your father's death," she said, "alone here in this great castle. My goodness, how forbidding it looked from the ship as we came into the harbor, standing there above us high on the headland, with all its towers soaring far into the foggy night. It reminded me of the Escorial."

"My father took pictures and drew plans of that palace before he built this one. He wanted Castillo Santiago to look like the Escorial."

"It does," Doña Octavia said, studying me for an instant, uncertain how far she should venture. "Philip the Second was quite mad, you know."

"I know."

"Did you ever think of your father as being somewhat mad himself?"

"Not until the last days. Not until the day we came upon the crystal caskets."

"But now you think so?"

I nodded.

"Poor child," Doña Octavia said, and for a few moments I thought she would put a protecting arm around me. "What you must have suffered! My heart goes out to you. I am so anxious about you. That is why I am here, Lucinda."

Her voice had grown dramatic, as if she were an actress on the stage, speaking lines in a play by Miguel de Cervantes Saavedra, throwing her words out to the last rows of the balcony.

Suddenly she said, "Do you know that Ricardo Villaverde is in Seville?"

"Yes."

"And that he came to see me?"

I had not been surprised when Father Martínez reported that Villaverde had flown to Spain. I had assumed he was there on business connected with my father's estate. But I *was* surprised that he had gone to see Doña Octavia.

"He came four days ago," she said. "Late at night, in a rainstorm, dripping wet. The butler thought he was a thug and wouldn't open the door until I heard the man say that he had just arrived from Isla del Oro with word that I would find important. What was I to do but let him in?" Doña Octavia sniffed. "So there he was, before I knew it, standing in my parlor, dripping water on my parquet floor."

"He came about the will?"

"Pulled it out of his pocket before he so much as sat down, and insisted that I read part of it."

She lowered her voice. "I asked him why he wanted me to. 'Because,' he said, 'I wish you to see that it is indeed the last will and testament of Don Enrique de Cabrillo y Benivides and that by it I am made the legal guardian of his daughter, Lucinda de Benivides.' "

"Did you read it?"

"Not at that moment. Remember how your father wrote — upside down and backwards."

"Did you believe Villaverde?"

"I couldn't imagine such a happening. Don Enrique was mad about most things, you know, but never about business. And the responsibility of being your guardian — with the . . . the men, the mines, and all that — *is* business, *enormous* business."

Waves were breaking on the rocks below the castle, and from far off I heard the drawn-out sighs of the whistling buoy on Punta del Norte. Doña Octavia heard the sounds too. They must have reminded her of the seas she had endured on her rough passage from the mainland, for she threw her arms about herself.

"Señor Villaverde is worried about you, Lucinda," she said. "He thinks you have never recovered from Don Enrique's passing."

Guttering in their sconces, candles sent out tendrils of smoke. (The servants responsible for replenishing the candles each day had become slack since my father's death.) One of the tendrils drifted across her face. She brushed it aside and gave me a lingering, gentle look.

"I know you will forgive me," she said, patting my arm, "if I repeat what Señor Villaverde told me about your life here in the castle, now that you are alone."

"What does Villaverde know about my life?" I said. "I don't confide in him or in anyone who does confide in him."

Doña Octavia smiled a motherly smile that showed teeth too perfect and white to be her own. "I am sure that all he says is quite wrong, though I have only known you through your letters to Porfirio and now from these brief moments together. I am very sure that you don't brood over Don Enrique's death. And that you don't have visions of him, as though

38

he were standing in the room right beside you."

Doña Octavia was lying. She did believe Villa-verde. She did believe that I sometimes had visions of my father. Since this was true, it didn't disturb me. Not nearly so much as a suspicion I detected in her voice — or was it from her impulse to stare at me whenever she thought I was not looking? — the suspicion that she felt I had inherited Don Enrique's madness.

"You did read the will?" I asked again.

"Only parts. Villaverde kept waving it in my face as he went on and on about how much he worried over you. Finally I asked to read it. He wouldn't give it up, but he led me into the hallway and held it to the mirror so I could read the words where Don Enrique refers to him as your legal guardian."

"That's all?"

"Except I did catch a glimpse of Don Enrique's signature. And it was his. I've seen his handwriting many times. The squiggly line sprawling across the page like a demented worm. But there's no reason to worry your head about Villaverde. He'll only be your guardian until the day you and Porfirio are married. What a wonderful day that will be! I —"

She was about to say more when a servant slipped in to replenish the guttering sconces. She fell silent and waited until he had snuffed out the old candles and lit fresh ones.

"How many servants do you have at Castillo Santiago?" she said. "There must be fifty. I have seen a dozen on my way here."

"Too many."

"I have three, and all of them are gossips. Are there any you can trust?"

"One."

"But now, Lucinda, now you have more." She kissed me on both my cheeks. "Two more!"

5.

Woman in Black

SEÑOR VILLAVERDE RETURNED FROM SEVILLE SIX days later. Fog hung over the harbor, but I saw him step ashore from the *Infanta,* at his side a tall woman dressed in black.

I looked for him to appear at the castle, but I didn't see him again until evening. Leaving the chapel after vespers, I was walking down the aisle, determined to ignore the window where my father knelt and prayed, when as I reached the door, a strong impulse forced me to glance up.

Villaverde stood there gazing down at me. He was dressed in a red doublet trimmed in lace, with white ruffs at his neck and wrists. I could make out only this much of him, but I could imagine the rest, for I had often seen my father dressed in this fashion — high-heeled shoes buckled in gold, silken, tight-fitting hose, a gold cane in his hand.

I recalled all this after one swift glance. Then the murky figure grew clear and changed before my eyes.

In place of Ricardo Villaverde looking down at me, I saw my father standing behind the golden screen. Hastily I turned away, swung open the heavy door, and stumbled out into the light.

Father Martínez overtook me before I reached the castle. "Villaverde," he said, "is not yet your legal guardian. However, in two or three months, depending on the courts, he will be. In the meantime, he has no authority over you, except what he can exert by persuasion and threats. Stand up to him, Lucinda."

"I shall."

"And Porfirio. He's had the castle in an uproar since several days ago when he arrived among us. Chasing the servants here and there for this and that. Complaining. Arrogant. I presume the arrogance got him his black eye somewhere on the journey."

"No, in Seville, his mother told me. Something awful happened to him there. She didn't say what."

"I can well imagine," Father Martínez said. "But he's your *novio*. You're betrothed to him. You'll need to be patient and forgiving. Remember, the last thing Villaverde wants is for you to marry Don Porfirio. And once he's your guardian, he can keep you from so doing until you reach the age of eighteen."

"What difference does it make? I'm duty-bound to follow my father's wishes. As soon as I'm eighteen, we'll be married."

"You sound like a besieged heroine from one of your Victorian novels. But whatever happens, remember to stand up to Don Porfirio. To Villaverde likewise. To both of them!"

42

Señor Villaverde had never sat down to a meal in Castillo Santiago except in the kitchen with the other servants, but on this night, to my great surprise, he appeared for dinner. With him was the tall, thin woman I had seen step off the ship.

"Señora Catalina de Portago," he said to me, "is a gentlewoman from the city of Toledo, from a family highly respected for its religious works. I have brought her here to be your adviser in matters of deportment and, I trust, a confidante in the mysterious ways of the heart."

In other words, Catalina de Portago was to be my duenna. She was to watch over me day and night, as if I were a child who didn't know right from wrong — or, knowing, wouldn't bother to choose one from the other. I'd had two nursemaids until I was nine, and tutors until I was nearly sixteen, but my father had never burdened me with a duenna. Now, for more than a year, I would be forced to endure a tall, thin shadow with a narrow face and prominent eyes the color of slate.

"How do you do?" I said, seething but smiling the best smile I could muster. I held out my hand, which she seized in a crushing grip, as though she were about to save me from drowning. "I hope you will find our way of life here on the island to your liking and not too different from your life in Toledo."

"I am fully prepared," she said. "Señor Villaverde has spoken to me."

"Señor Villaverde is not the most reliable of sources about life on Isla del Oro," I said, thinking it best to start on an honest footing. "Señor Villaverde, like you, is from Toledo, which I judge from my reading to be one of the most religious of Spanish cities. It was the home of El Greco — we have two of his paintings of Christ. And was it not one of the centers for the Inquisition? What I am trying to say is, no matter what you have been told, Isla del Oro is not Toledo and while Señor Villaverde will one day be my guardian, now he neither breathes for me nor tells me how to comb my hair."

Catalina de Portago looked at me in silence down her long, thin nose, which was pointed like a stiletto. She was silent, for she had a headful of instructions and she intended to carry them out. It is said that still waters run deep, but with Catalina de Portago, as I was to learn, the water was not deep — just stagnant, a pool of prejudice and envy.

Villaverde placed her next to me at table and seated himself in the carved ebony chair with the tasseled cushion where my father always sat. He was wearing a different costume from the one I had seen him in a few hours before. Most elaborate and formal, it came from the ancient time when Pizarro returned to Spain and Inca gold poured into the country. It was a costume that my father wore at special times. On either side of Villaverde squatted my father's gray staghounds.

Don Porfirio sat at the foot of the table and two places away sat Doña Octavia. The Puertoblancos hadn't appeared that day, taking their meals in their rooms. Doña Octavia had made no requests, but Porfirio had had two servants running back and forth to the kitchen from the time he had awakened at noon. And Panchito drove his carriage once to the village for sundries and once to the *Infanta* with an urgent message Porfirio wished sent to Seville on the ship-to-shore radio.

Father Martínez, who sat next to Señor Villaverde, asked if his visit to Seville had been a pleasant one. Villaverde hesitated before answering, plainly surprised that Father Martínez knew where he had been.

"More than pleasant," he said. "It was of unusual significance. Of historical grandeur."

Doña Octavia was talking at the far end of the table to Salvador Zoyo, superintendent of our mines. Villaverde waited until she ceased, until the servants quit rattling silverware, until I laid down my fork.

Then, in an imitation of my father's sepulchral tones, he said, "During my visit to Spain, I came upon a document hidden among a bundle of dusty papers in one of Don Enrique's storehouses. It had lain there for centuries."

The vast room was silent, except for the soughing of the *chubasco* and a peal of far-off thunder. The staghounds rose at the sound and went to the windows. There were six windows — huge leaded panes that extended from the floor to the high ceiling. The hounds trotted to each of the windows, listened, and then returned to their places beside Villaverde's chair.

"Hidden from the eyes of Don Enrique," he continued. "Hidden, alas, from that great Spanish patriot. How he would have responded to the discovery! I can see his face now, lifted to the heavens in prayerful exaltation."

Villaverde's voice had grown thick. He paused and his eyes misted over. "I will reveal no more at this time," he said, overcome with emotion.

"You have us on tiptoes," Father Martínez said. "What did you find that has such immense historical significance? I will make a guess. You discovered a code that unlocks the secrets of the hieroglyphic writings on the temples of the ancient Maya. Like the Rosetta Stone, which unlocked the secrets of ancient Egypt, this will tell us, tell me as an astronomer, how the Maya Indians calculated sidereal time — time based upon the observations of the stars. How with no instruments at their command, only a slit in a stone tower, they came within seconds of our own time, which is calculated by the most refined telescopes. Have you by any chance, *señor,* discovered such a code?"

Villaverde frowned, suspicious. Was Father Martínez making fun?

Salvador Zoyo was the next to join the guessing game. "You discovered a map, sir. It was drawn by Don Aurelio on that day he found the gold pebble in Playa Blanca. It shows different veins from those we mine now."

Villaverde smiled. It was very difficult for him. His mouth tilted to one side and opened like a trap, so slowly it seemed to creak.

Porfirio, who had sat gloomily silent at table, said, "Could it be, Señor Villaverde, that you have discovered why this room is lit by electricity, by more candelabra than are found at the king's palace in Madrid, while on the upper floors, in my handsome quarters, one gropes around by the light of candles? And worse yet, there's no connection for my razor, which runs on electricity, and without electricity not at all."

He laughed — perhaps to take the edge off the rude remark — displaying beautiful white teeth, so white against his tanned skin.

"Why don't you grow a beard?" I said. "Then you wouldn't need to shave."

"I'll have to," he replied. "Do you prefer any particular shape?"

Doña Octavia said, "A beard that makes two graceful curves on either side of his face and joins together in a small, pointed tuft would become him, don't you think, Lucinda?"

I screwed up my mouth in a critical gesture and said, "Perhaps two points would suit him better."

Her son laughed again, but he was not in a happy mood.

"Unfortunately," Octavia said, "Porfirio has a machine to dry his hair and another for massages."

I glanced at the man sitting proudly in my father's chair, resplendent in his courtly costume. "Señor Villaverde shaved my father twice each day," I said, "in the morning and before dinner at night. He would be pleased to render similar services for Don Porfirio, I am certain."

I meant these words to remind Villaverde that he was an intruder. He took them as such, with no

47

change of expression. Once again the servant, he said, "For Don Porfirio this will be an honor."

"You are very thoughtful," Doña Octavia said. "I know that Don Porfirio will be pleased. I haven't made my guess yet," she went on. "What will it be, Porfirio?"

He shrugged.

Catalina de Portago, sitting stiffly in her high-backed chair, said nothing.

"And you, Lucinda, what is your guess?" Villaverde asked.

"I guess this, *señor*. You have discovered that you are a half-brother of my father, Don Enrique. And to celebrate the discovery you have dressed up to resemble him."

My gibe must have caused him some anguish, but there was no sign of it on his bony face, nothing except the beginning of another painful smile. I looked for him to draw the document from his coat and brandish it before us, but in a quiet voice he informed us that it was now with the House of Contracts in Seville.

His voice rose. "This beautiful island that once flew the flag of Spain will fly it once again. The document proves that on the infamous day when the *gringos* conquered California, they did not conquer our island. By a glorious circumstance Isla del Oro remained in Spain's possession. And so it remains today. Tomorrow we raise the Spanish flag on all four towers."

In alarm at his ringing words, the staghounds jumped to their feet and sniffed the air.

48

6.

A Discreet Spy

BY EVENING OF THE NEXT DAY, FOUR BLACK AND gold flags flew from the towers of Castillo Santiago. A strong south wind blowing in from Mexico whipped the flags straight out, so they looked more like pieces of painted wood than cloth.

"Do you like the flags?" Porfirio asked Father Martínez as we left the chapel after the evening service. "To me they mean nothing."

"Nothing save trouble," Father Martínez said. "After all these years of Mexican and American rule, it's not likely that Spain can claim Isla del Oro. But should the courts rule otherwise?"

"Then the king takes over Isla del Oro. The island, the castle, the mines — everything. Oh, they might leave us the castle. It could become a fine place for sightseers. We could charge admission and serve tea on the terrace as noble lords and ladies do now in England."

49

I was interested in how glibly he spoke of "we," including himself in the fate of the island, taking for granted that Lucinda de Benivides would be his wife. It was difficult to remember that I was engaged to Porfirio Puertoblanco, that he was my *novio,* that the contract between our families had been solemnly sealed long years ago.

"You're making fun of Villaverde," I said to him, "but he is like my father. He would rather see Castillo Santiago crashing down stone by stone than give up this wild idea."

"Crashing around our ears," Father Martínez said, stopping to pick up a copper tile that the wind had pried from one of the towers.

"Forty miles south of us are the Coronados," I said. "They belong to Mexico. If Villaverde proves that Spain owns our island, then Mexico will make a counterclaim based upon the treaty it signed with Spain in eighteen hundred and twenty-one, which gave them all the Spanish territories in the Southwest. Then where will we be?"

"I have friends in the Spanish ministry," Porfirio said. "They will put an end to Villaverde's nonsense." He spoke with authority, striking the air with his fist. "I will warn him that he's asking for trouble."

Villaverde wore different clothes to dinner that night, an elaborate costume of ruffs and lace and yellow, tight-fitting boots of shiny cordovan and a dagger on a delicate chain. He did not mention the deed he had found, but to my surprise asked if I objected to his taking his place at the head of the table, in my father's chair.

"Last night it seemed to displease you," he said. "Perhaps you thought I was a bold pretender, making a clumsy effort to imitate your father and assume his awesome powers. No man could ever do this. Do you think that I, his devoted servant, his worshipful friend, would be so ill-advised as to try?"

I saw no sign on his secretive face that he felt humble or was experiencing the least discomfort. In his imagination he had sat at Don Enrique's place a thousand times before.

"I know that you are not that ill-advised, *señor,* so sit where you please and do me the kind favor of asking Portago to stop treading on my heels. This morning when I went to the beach for a swim I saw her watching me from the terrace. Later, in the chapel, she was eavesdropping behind me while I knelt at the confessional."

We were standing in the small family room, waiting for our guests to go in to dinner. The walls were covered with portraits. Most of them had been painted of my father, showing him as a sailor on the deck of the *Infanta;* a hunter poised with one foot resting on the carcass of a mountain lion; a scientist in smock and goggles doing something over a tiny flame; and a scholar seated at his library desk, stacks of books piled on the floor. The largest of the portraits, hung in the most prominent place, showed him in a miner's hat with its lamp burning brightly and a pickax in his hand, a gloved hand.

Villaverde glanced up at the portraits. "You complain of being spied upon," he said. "My first day on Isla del Oro — it was long before you were born — I went to your father's workshop at the smelter. I found him working on an experiment — I believe it had something to do with the lost secret of Damascene steel he was trying to rediscover. In any event, he was deeply absorbed, so I stood quietly at the door until he had finished. Looking up to find me there, he flew into a tirade, cursed me roundly, accused me of coming to spy upon him. Down the years he grew more and more suspicious. It became a disease with him — as you know."

He shifted his gaze and fixed it upon me. His eyes were barely visible beneath their half-closed lids, yet I could not miss the light that shone there. Edgar Allan Poe would have called it "a baleful fire." In less melodramatic words, it was a light that chilled me.

"You are a strong-willed girl," he said. "It's not easy to take advice, but you must. You must do everything that lies within your power to heed this warning. Do not, I repeat, do not follow Don Enrique, brilliant though he was and a great patriot, down the way that led to his death."

His eyes bored into me. I didn't look away but met them. They willed me to believe that I had already taken my father's tortuous path. And more, that nothing could ever save me from his fate.

Villaverde sadly shook his head. "I assure you that Doña Catalina only seeks your happiness. But I will

52

caution her to remember that you are not yet recovered from Don Enrique's untimely death."

At the table, more interested in Doña Octavia than in the duenna, he asked her if she had given thought to a date for her son's marriage.

"Hours of thought," she replied. "I have always favored spring weddings — April is a romantic month. Is it a pleasant month on the island?"

"It is pleasant, but at least a year of mourning must be observed," Villaverde said.

Doña Octavia raised her thick brows. "I am aware that this is the Spanish custom, *señor,* but in the circumstance custom must bow to necessity. Lucinda is not happy living without the love of mother or father, alone here in a vast castle of bitter memories. We cannot ask this of her. It's inhuman."

"Lucinda is not alone," Villaverde said defiantly. "She's surrounded by crowds of servants and people. Father Martínez is here. The Vegas are here. I am here. You and your son are here. Now she has another friend." He glanced down the table at Catalina de Portago. "A friend ever mindful of her. Discreetly so."

These last words were not lost upon the duenna. She betrayed no emotion other than a slight tightening of her lips, but when Porfirio and I went to the music room after dinner she followed us at a discreet distance.

7.

Conversation at the Harpsichord

CEREMONIOUSLY, AS IF IT WERE A SWORD AND I A SERvant, Porfirio handed me his cane.

With a few quiet groans he arranged himself on the music bench, a spindly piece that might collapse under his weight at any moment. I told him so but he sat there anyway, stretching his arms, flexing his fingers, tapping his good foot — showing off.

He turned to fix me with the eye that didn't sport a patch. "What, Lucinda de Cabrillo y Benivides, do you think about my mother's marriage plans?"

"I haven't thought about them at all," I said at once, speaking the truth.

"Neither have I." He ran his fingers over the keys and made a discord — on purpose, it seemed, to match his mood. "What do you think of marriages arranged by parents without consulting their offspring?"

"Barbaric," I said blithely.

"Like the marriage contracts parents used to make in India. Perhaps they still do. Between twelve-year-olds."

"In other places, too."

"Backward places," Porfirio said. Then he played a short piece — rather well, I thought — and asked me if I had formed any opinions of him during the years we had been engaged. I shook my head.

"You must have had a thought or two."

He goaded me into saying, "Judging from the pictures your father sent, I thought you would be fat."

"And judging from reports, I thought you would be spoiled."

"I'm not, as you can see."

"Not much," Porfirio said, "not considering how rotten spoiled you could have been." He began a romantic folk tune and stopped in the middle of it to say, "Probably you think that I am marrying you for your money."

"You must have had thoughts about the matter at some time during our long engagement."

"Stray thoughts."

He spoke flippantly, as Hernán Cortés, the conquistador, might have spoken to one of Moctezuma's numerous wives — arrogantly, in the true spirit of Spanish *machismo*. He was arrogant as my father, I decided.

"Stray thoughts, if any," he said again.

I didn't believe him for a second, not a word. "To put your mind at rest," I said, "we have three mines, Mine Number One, Mine Number Two, and Mine

Number Three. They produce all together an average of twelve thousand *onzas* of gold each week, which is shipped to the mint in gold bars. Gold is now selling for around four hundred and ten dollars an ounce."

I expected to see his brow furrowed in thought as he computed the worth of twelve thousand gold ounces, but he was gazing at a portrait on the wall.

"Who is the young lady with the smile?" he asked.

"Teresa de Benivides."

"A relative?"

"Yes."

He stopped playing. "You both have the same smile."

I recalled Tolstoi's description of Princess Lisa Bolkónskaya. "Her pretty little upper lip," he wrote, "on which a delicate dark brown was just perceptible, was too short for her teeth, but it lifted all the more sweetly and was especially charming when she occasionally drew it down to meet the lower lip." I remembered, but didn't take the trouble to explain, that it wasn't a smile we shared, only the way our mouths were made.

"Curious," he said, "and rather charming. The painting looks very old. The girl is dead?"

"For three hundred years."

"How sad."

I was silent and he was too. Then he motioned me to hand him his cane. "The ankle's better," he said.

"I thought it was your leg."

"The ankle is part of the leg," he said. "They're connected one to the other and they both hurt. You

56

have never asked me how it happened. I nearly lost my life."

"I thought you'd be embarrassed if I did ask."

"I revel in telling people how it all happened. I have told the story many times. Each time it comes out a little different."

"What is the latest version?"

"Well, this is the truth, word for word," Porfirio said. "I guess you know that I've been at the university for three years now, studying metallurgy. Just a week before we came here, I left an evening lecture and went out the south entrance with an armful of notebooks and papers."

Porfirio took a deep breath.

"It was about ten-thirty then. The university was once the palace of San Telmo, one of the biggest buildings in Spain, and it has a deep moat around it and numerous crannies. Suddenly out of one of the crannies a band of thugs appeared — the night was dark and I couldn't see how many, perhaps five. Without a sound, without a word, they fell upon me from all sides. I didn't have time to call for help. The struggle was brief. I was beaten over the head, picked up bodily, and thrown into the moat, which had no water in it. I lay there unconscious through the night and until the following noon, barely more alive than dead, shall we say."

"Did they ever find the thugs?"

"Not by the time I left Seville. But they'll find them one of these days. The day I went back to my studies, they had me come down to the police station to identify a suspect. He turned out to be a classmate I had quarreled with. I had handed in a term paper on mercury mining at Almadén. The Almadén mines were discovered and worked by the Romans. That long ago. He had turned in a paper on the same subject and . . ."

"I didn't know you were studying such things at the university," I said.

"But I wrote you about them three years ago. And you found the news so exciting that you promptly forgot."

Which I had. "What happened to your classmate?" I asked.

"Nothing. He presented the police with an alibi and two of the professors backed it up."

Porfirio got to his feet, leaned hard on his cane, and went off without a word.

8.

Smoke

After I had said goodnight to Catalina de Portago and Doña Octavia — Porfirio had gone straight to bed, hobbling up the winding stairs, stopping to call down the stairwell at the top of his voice, "When do we install an elevator? This is like climbing the Alps!" — I decided to find a book to read in bed, something that would put me fast asleep.

I hadn't been near my father's library since the night he died, when I had gone there searching for him. Repelled by the awful threats I had heard in the room, by the desperate plans discussed, by the blasphemies uttered, by the memory of the fire that had turned his last testament into ashes, I hated to go there now. But I had read everything in my own library — all of Poe and Scott and Balzac — twice.

Halfway down the passageway to the library I became certain I was being followed, probably by Catalina de Portago. The birds in the aviary set up a commotion. I turned about and retraced my steps. She was sitting in the music room beside Doña Octavia, where I had left her.

As I opened the library door I was met by an acrid smell, which I recognized at once as coming from the special brand of cigar my father smoked — a flat, pale variety made for him in Spain. The room hasn't been aired in a month or more, I told myself. It is stale smoke that I smell. Then I saw that a dead cigar, half-smoked, lay in the ashtray.

A cluster of a hundred tear-shaped bulbs hung from the ceiling. But none of the lights was burning. The only light came from an oil lamp at one side of the desk — the right side, because Don Enrique wrote with his left hand, and in this position the lamp didn't cast shadows on the page.

The lamp shed a weak circle of light around the desk. Pale light fell on its gleaming black surface, on holders stuffed with quill pens, and on his mammoth inkwell, which was shaped like Cabrillo's caravel. Its three deep hatches were filled with red and black and violet ink — colors to suit my father's changing moods — and its lookout tower held the odd-shaped object my grandfather had found rolling idly back and forth with the tide: the golden pebble, no larger than a pea, that had led him to the richest mines in the world and had made his son, Don Enrique de Cabrillo y Benivides, the world's richest man.

I went over to the wall and turned on the light switches, one after the other. They made soft sounds, but the cluster of bulbs overhead did not go on.

I peered into the shadowy recesses. Nothing had changed. Books — thousands of them — were there in dark, forbidding rows behind leaded-glass doors that were closed and locked.

The keys were kept in a lower drawer of the desk. I found them but in my nervousness dropped them on the floor. As I reached down, my hand touched the back of my father's chair. I saw with horror that the imprint of his body was clearly visible on the scarlet cushions.

I flung the keys on the desk and ran toward the hallway. Before I reached it the cluster overhead flashed on, flooding the library with brilliant light. In an open door at the end of the room I caught a fleeting glimpse of a figure in a peaked hat trimmed with feathers, a hat like one my father sometimes wore.

I must have screamed, for as I ran into the hall and down the long passageway, past the aviary, startled birds again set up a clatter. I ran blindly into the outstretched arms of Doña Octavia. She put her hand over my mouth to silence me.

"Whatever has happened?" she gasped.

"Nothing," I said.

"But you're shaking."

I grasped her by the hand and led her back down the passageway. In the library the smell of cigar smoke seemed stronger.

"What?" Doña Octavia said, and said it over and over until I pointed at the desk, gleaming under the flood of lights.

"The ashtray," I said.

She glanced at me, uncomprehending. I stepped to the desk, pulling her along. Again I pointed at the ashtray. As I did so, I saw that it was empty. There was nothing in the tray, not even ashes.

Doña Octavia was silent. Our eyes met. "My dear child," she said in the gentlest of voices, "I know how you feel. Your father's death has been a terrible blow." She patted my arm. "Come, I'll put you to bed."

Doña Catalina must have followed us down the passageway. She must have stood outside the door, alert, and heard everything that was said, for she appeared at once.

"Lucinda is my responsibility," she said. "I will see that she is cared for. We will go now, if you will permit us."

Doña Octavia's broad figure blocked the doorway. The two women silently confronted each other. I slipped around them both and ran. I didn't stop running until I reached the tower and closed the door and bolted it behind me.

Soon afterward I heard a soft knock. Then a louder knock. The third knock I answered by asking who was there, although I knew. I could hear her hard breathing through the six inches of oak door.

"Kindly let me in," Doña Catalina said. "I wish to have a word with you."

"I am going to bed."

"Only for a minute."

"We can talk tomorrow."

9.

"Through Caverns
Measureless to Man"

THE FOLLOWING DAY I BROKE THE APPOINTMENT
Doña Catalina had made for me with Dr. Beltrán. I
stayed in the tower with the door bolted, not answering her knock, refusing to eat, and sleeping most
of the time.

By the second day, having gotten hold of myself, I
went down to dinner. Dr. Beltrán was there as a guest
of Señor Villaverde, bowing as we met and compli-
menting me on the pink dress I wore.

Tall and thin with a black beard and dark, heavy-
lidded eyes, he reminded me of a picture I had once
seen of a Christianized Moor from medieval Spain. In
a scarlet turban and a flowing white gown, Dr. Beltrán
would have been the exact picture of a dashing
Mudéjar.

He was a grave young man — bowing his head in
some sort of obeisance before he ate — and silent,
seemingly absorbed in his own thoughts. From time

to time during dinner, however, I caught his eyes fixed upon me.

After dinner, while I sat at the harpsichord, he invited me to visit the village hospital, where mine injuries were treated and pills passed out to the servants. Wives of the miners had their babies at home and only went to the hospital, and then reluctantly, when there was an emergency or a serious illness.

"I found it in bad shape," Dr. Beltrán said.

"Dr. Wolfe was concerned with other things," I let him know.

"Yes, Señor Villaverde told me about the experiments she made. Horrible. And on ten women."

I corrected him. "Eighteen."

"I've cleaned up all evidence of Dr. Wolfe," he said. "I would like you to see what I've done. And what my plans are for the future."

"I'll come to visit you," I said, but as I made this promise I had a strong suspicion that his invitation was only a ruse to lure me into the hospital so that he could close the door and talk and talk, probing me with all sorts of personal questions.

"When can I expect you?" he asked, looking at me for a long time from beneath his half-closed lids. "Soon?"

"As soon as I see to certain matters, Dr. Beltrán."

One of the matters was the future of the nineteen caskets, eighteen of which had held the remains of the *gringas*. The coroner's assistants had gathered them up when the murders were investigated and stored them in the basement of the chapel. Having a sensational history and therefore being of interest to the morbid, they had brought a number of requests from showmen who wished to exhibit them. To one — a Mr. Simpson of Simpson and Simpson, a firm in San Francisco — I agreed to sell the nineteen caskets.

Mr. Simpson was to arrive on the *Infanta* at the end of the week. I was anxious to see him, to be rid of the caskets, to know that they were not anywhere on the island. And since Villaverde was not yet my guardian, I said nothing to him about the negotiations.

Mr. Simpson arrived late Saturday afternoon with his daughter, Emily. He spoke with what seemed to be an English accent — at least it was not the American, *gringo* accent I had heard before — and was a small, fat man with patches of bright red color on his cheeks. Emily, also fat, whom I took to be no older than ten, had her father's blue eyes and pretty coloring.

The day was quite warm. I had tea for them on the terrace overlooking the sea, and invited Doña Catalina and Porfirio and his mother to join us. Our chef was good at baking French pastries, although he was a native of Madrid, and truly wonderful with cakes. He made us a sacher torte, from the recipe of the famous restaurant keeper who fed the impoverished Austrian nobility years after they had ceased to pay, and, besides the torte, two lovely cakes: a mocha chiffon and an almond Cockaigne in seven layers with chocolate butter icing.

Mr. Simpson ate heartily of all three, but Emily, who had read about the murders on Isla del Oro and seen pictures of the island and its castle, was so excited that she only picked at the great gob of cream, white schlag that topped her torte. She no sooner sat down at the table than she whispered in my ear, wanting to know where the crystal caskets were kept and when we were going to see them.

At dusk the five of us — Doña Octavia having decided that she did not wish to see the caskets, that the very thought of them made her ill — strolled toward the chapel in the failing light.

Mr. Simpson was carrying on a conversation with Doña Catalina, limited by their unfamiliarity with each other's language. Fat little Emily had me tightly by the hand and made unintelligible sounds compounded of fear and delight. Porfirio limped along on his cane, probably fearing that all was a waste of time.

As we reached the chapel door everyone fell silent. There were no lights in the basement, so I took three candles from the vestibule and gave one to Porfirio. Before I started down, I glanced up at the screened window. There was no sign of Villaverde or the staghounds.

The descent into the basement was steep — two flights of stairs cut into the bare rock, the stairs wet underfoot, and the black walls glistening with moisture. I went in the lead, holding the two candles, cautioning my guests against the slippery stairs.

"Is this the first circle of Dante's Hell?" Porfirio asked. His words echoed through the cavernous room, then died away in a series of whispers. No one answered him.

In the dim candlelight the basement looked empty.

I held my candles as high as I could, and Porfirio limped forward with his. Their light penetrated into the farthest corners. The room, indeed, was empty. Mr. Simpson gave a polite gasp of surprise and disappointment. Emily began to sniffle. Doña Catalina drew in her breath. She stood behind me and I couldn't see her face. Porfirio said, "Is this a joke?"

I was embarrassed. "Not more than a week ago, the caskets were right over there. In two rows between the pillars."

As I pointed, a white shape fluttered in the darkness. At first I thought it might be one of the white bats that frequented parts of the castle. Then I looked closer and saw that it was a small paper, astir in the fetid air.

Thinking that it might have something to do with the missing caskets, I asked the others to remain where they were while I investigated. The paper was taped to the first pillar. As I shone the candlelight upon it, before I could make out that it contained a message, I was seized with foreboding. My heart began to pound.

The message was written in script, from margin to margin, upside down and from right to left, and in violet ink. My father's handwriting!

The message, the note — whatever it was — couldn't be deciphered without a mirror. I ripped it from the pillar, hid it in my bodice, and said nothing about it when I rejoined the guests.

"The caskets have been moved," I said. "Let me find out where they are."

I left the group in the chapel with Father Martínez and took the stairs to the servants' parlor, the closest place where I could find a mirror. The room was crowded with servants chattering over their afternoon chocolate. Everyone stopped to stare at me. Quickly I turned away and ran up the stairs to the third floor.

A dozen mirrors decorated the long passageway. Candles hadn't been lighted yet. It was too dark to read. The door to Alicia's room was open and the mirror above her bureau shone with the last of the westering sun, but at the same instant I saw her shadow lying across the bed.

I ran to the end of the passage and up the stairs to my tower and bolted the door behind me. Holding a match to the candles on either side of the mirror, unfolding the crumpled paper, I read in the flickering light:

> *In Xanadu did Kubla Khan*
> *A stately pleasure-dome decree:*
> *Where Alph, the sacred river, ran*
> *Through caverns measureless to man*
> *Down to a sunless sea.*
> *. . . But oh! that deep romantic chasm which*
>   *slanted*
> *Down the green hill athwart a cedarn cover!*
> *A savage place! As holy and enchanted*
> *As e'er beneath a waning moon was haunted*
> *By woman wailing for her demon-lover!*

I recognized the words. They were the beginning of a Coleridge poem that my father liked, but what did it mean? Certainly, it didn't explain why the caskets had been moved or where they were. But did it portend? Was the poem a cryptic message?

Not stopping to think — I had been away from my guests for ten minutes at least — I left the paper on the bed and took a shortcut back to the chapel, through the gallery and the Great Hall. I still didn't know where the caskets had been moved to, but on a chance I took the impatient group down two flights of stairs, past the tombs of Juan Cabrillo and the obscure Nayarit Indian whose bones were posing as those of Gaspar de Portolá, and through the dark, seemingly endless tunnel.

The crypt's gold-banded doors were ajar. Emily, who had bravely led the party through the tunnel, if only by one hesitant step, put an eye to the opening. Then she let out a chilling scream and clutched my hand. Her father thought that she had seen enough and, not reluctantly, Emily went back with Doña Catalina to the chapel.

Mr. Simpson and Porfirio followed me into the crypt. A thin layer of scented smoke lay from wall to wall above the nineteen caskets, which sat in the same neat row I had seen them in during my last brief visit. Votive candles also sat in the same deep niches, casting an amber glow upon the marble walls, which sent the same waves of amber light cascading through the room.

Mr. Simpson said, "God in Heaven!" Crossing himself, Porfirio was silent.

The nameplate at the foot of the first casket read as

71

it had read before — "Margaret Drew." She of the rosebud mouth, the flaring nostrils, the small pink ears that nestled close to her head, the broad brow, and the long black lashes curving down over her closed eyes.

The second casket had held the body of the girl who looked like one of Raphael's madonnas. The other caskets, I assumed, were in their ordered places, just as they had been before, in the exact sequence of their owners' deaths.

Mr. Simpson had taken out his pen and was strolling along the row making notes on a pad.

At that instant the verse from "Kubla Khan" flashed before my eyes: "... the sacred river ran / Through caverns measureless to man / Down to a sunless sea." I still did not understand what they were supposed to mean. Had the caskets been returned to the crypt to inform me that life on Isla del Oro must go on as it had in the past?

Mr. Simpson was making notes beside the last of the caskets, when I heard a faint rustling. I knew at once that it was the sound the bushmaster made when it was sliding along on the marble floor. Scarcely a sound, more of a drawn-out whisper.

I held my breath, not knowing how close the serpent was to Mr. Simpson, whether to frighten him by a shout, or whether he was even in danger. Then the slithering faded away in a far corner of the crypt and Mr. Simpson, having completed his inspection, came back to where Porfirio and I stood.

"The caskets are all alike," he said. "They are made of the purest silicon dioxide. The plaques, I assume, are all twenty-two-carat gold." He glanced at his notes. "I am prepared to offer you thirty thousand dollars for each of the nineteen."

At that instant, as he put the notes in his pocket, the words of the message came back to me. Now they had an ominous sound. Suddenly I saw them there in front of me, written on the marble wall in letters of fire.

"Thirty thousand dollars," Mr. Simpson said. "A very handsome offer."

Porfirio said, "It seems reasonable."

"I have . . ."

Mr. Simpson spoke again before I had finished, thinking that I was trying to strike a bargain. "Thirty-one thousand, Miss Benivides."

"You don't understand."

"For a grand total of five hundred and eighty-nine thousand dollars. The caskets to be delivered on the wharf in San Francisco."

Speaking calmly, I said, "The caskets are not for sale."

"Six hundred thousand," Mr. Simpson offered.

"They are not for sale at any price," I said. "Sorry, I should have told you long before this. Before you came. I'll gladly pay you for your time."

I was surprised when Mr. Simpson did not utter a word. But before he turned away and we started back down the dark tunnel, he looked at me in a curious way, almost sadly, as much as to say, "I am sorry, too, for both of us, and someday I'll come back when you are in better health."

Porfirio and I took the Simpsons to the harbor and saw them safely aboard the *Infanta,* Emily with the cakes she hadn't so much as sampled. Then I went back to the castle. The paper was not in my room where I had put it. Thinking it possible that I hadn't left it on the bed, that I had lost it somewhere on the way, I retraced my steps down the long stairway, through the gallery and the Great Hall, as far as the chapel. To no avail.

At dinner I could think of nothing but the cryptic message. Afterwards, when I sat down to the harpsichord at Doña Octavia's request, I made a botch of both Rameau and Bach. The little wooden keys froze stiff under my cold fingers. A log was smoldering in the fireplace. Angry at myself, I asked the servants to throw my harpsichord in the fire, and I hurried away, leaving them to ponder my grim joke.

Again I searched the tower. I looked everywhere, but the message was not to be found. I read the Bible for a while, trying to calm myself, then the happy scenes in *Jane Eyre,* my favorite book, but when I dozed off the scenes vanished, and in their place I was in a ruined tower, a haunt of bats and owls, with a shape much like the one Jane described standing stark before her:

"Fearful and ghastly . . . I never saw a face like it. It was a discolored face — a savage face. I wish I could forget the roll of the red eyes . . . the lips were swelled and dark; the brow furrowed; the black eyebrows widely raised over the bloodshot eyes . . ."

Not once during the long hours before dawn did a happy scene appear before me. I did not leave the tower for two days. Then I went out in the afternoon of the third day and walked along the beach until dusk. When I returned to the tower, the fears that had haunted me since the moment I found the mysterious note, the strange poem written in my father's spidery hand, had vanished.

10.

The Arab

THAT NIGHT THE BEAUTIFUL QUETZAL BIRD PERCHED on my window ledge and sang its thrushlike melodies. I took it as a good omen. For days now I had seen a pair of hawks circling the tower, so I decided as I listened to the quetzal's song to have the bird netted and put in a cage in one of the nearby rooms, where it would be safe from the hunters.

The next morning I went to see Dr. Beltrán.

I had not been in the office since Gerda Wolfe was our doctor. It was very plain then, with bare white walls and a plain rug woven of reeds — as cold as the woman who sat behind the metal desk.

Dr. Beltrán, to suit his Moorish background, had redecorated the office in the Mudéjar style. There were pale purple curtains at the windows, and the four walls were painted a golden yellow, decorated with crossed spears, and hung with four large Oriental tapestries depicting harem scenes and battles. Underfoot was a Persian rug from the palace of Sultan Rashid Haroum, borrowed from my father's storerooms like all of the things, including the black ebony desk where Dr. Beltrán, as I was ushered in, sat smoking a cigarette.

He got to his feet and, crushing out his cigarette, asked me to be seated. The chair faced him and the window at his back, and when I sat down the sun shone squarely in my eyes. It was like having a strong lamp shining on me.

"I didn't expect you this soon," Dr. Beltrán said. "I am glad you decided not to delay our talk. You are a healthy young specimen, so for now I'll not take time to examine your heart and so forth. We'll just talk."

Dr. Beltrán was dressed in a purple robe with a stiff embroidered collar that came up to his chin and long, flowing sleeves that he kept pushing back. The robe and his heavy-lidded eyes and tawny skin made him look more and more like one of the ancient Mudéjars whom my ancestors had driven from Spain centuries ago — to Spain's great misfortune, for many of the Mudéjars were brilliant scholars. There was a scholarly look about Dr. Beltrán that I began to like as he sat there studying me, smiling faintly, as if my presence gave him pleasure.

"Shall we lay aside formalities and leap into the heart of things?" he said. "I am informed that you have been deeply affected by the death of your father. And yet when he was alive, so I am told by Señor Villaverde, there were many arguments that ended in violent threats. On one occasion your father even disowned you and burned his will."

A white-clad nurse came in and handed Dr. Beltrán a note, which he placed on the table and didn't read. The nurse gave me a searching glance when she went out and smiled, as much as to say, "I am glad and everyone else on the island is glad that Lucinda de Cabrillo y Benivides has come to the doctor for help."

Dr. Beltrán said, "But for all the quarrels and violence, you were strongly attached to your father. You still are. But it was an ambivalent feeling. By ambivalent I mean . . ."

"I understand, Dr. Beltrán, the meaning of ambivalent." It was a rude remark that just slipped out, spoken before I thought.

Undismayed, the doctor went on. "One day you hated your father, the next day you loved him."

"Those things are in the past," I said.

"The past is present, Miss Lucinda. With most of us, no matter how hard we try to forget."

He must have seen that I was uncomfortable with the sun streaming into my face. He must have wondered why I didn't complain. It occurred to me that he wanted me to feel uncomfortable. But perhaps I was wrong, because the very next moment he asked if the sun was a bother.

"Not at all," I said, "thank you."

Gently, in a soft Castilian accent that had a trace of Mudéjar in it, he said, "The night before last, I believe it was, you went into your father's library and smelled cigar smoke. You noticed a dead cigar lying in the ashtray on the desk. Then you saw your father sitting in his chair."

"He wasn't in his chair," I said. "But I saw the fresh prints of his body. He had been there recently and gone."

"Then you never really saw him?"

"Not really."

"But you're certain that he had been in the library," Dr. Beltrán said. "Was this the first encounter?"

"No," I said and described the things that had happened to me on the day I decided to leave the island, then changed my mind at the last minute. "Yesterday I received a message from my father. In his handwriting."

"I hear that his writing is very difficult — that you need a mirror to read it," Dr. Beltrán said.

He was listening closer now, his dark eyes fixed upon me, as I told him what had taken place in the basement, how the caskets had disappeared and I had found the message and taken it to the tower.

"After I read the message, I left it on the bed, thinking to read it again when Mr. Simpson had gone, but when I went back I couldn't find it."

Dr. Beltrán got up, turned on the lamps that stood at either end of his desk, closed the curtains, picked up the note the nurse had given him, and, excusing himself with a bow, left the room.

The lamps had tall brass stems crowned by yellow shades hung with colored beads. They gave off a pale mixture of yellow and blue light. The desk was bare except for an odd paperweight, one of the shrunken heads found along the Amazon. A tenth of its original size, no larger than an apple, the head had kept all of its human features — the ridged brow, the flaring nose, the tawny Indian color, even a shock of coarse black hair that enveloped the little face and flowed out upon the desk. The eye sockets were in shadow, but did I see something in them? Were these the eyes of a girl that looked out at me silently, in fear and foreboding?

When Dr. Beltrán came back, he sat down and began to tap on the desk. His fingers were very white and without rings. He tapped softly and studied me for a while, an amused look on his face.

Suddenly he said, "Do you consider yourself an intelligent being?"

"Sometimes I wonder."

"You *are* intelligent," he said, "and being intelligent, I wonder how you can possibly believe that your father wanders about, sits in his library smoking cigars, and leaves messages here and there."

Not a question, this was an exclamation of polite but utter doubt. I didn't try to answer.

"Has anyone besides you seen Don Enrique? Doña Catalina hasn't. She informs me that there was not one sign of your father anywhere in the library. There wasn't, because your father is dead. The dead, Miss Lucinda, do not send handwritten messages to the living."

I avoided his eyes. The passage from "Kubla Khan" stood between us, as clear as the moment my father had written it down in his tortuous hand —

80

"Where Alph, the sacred river, ran / Through caverns measureless to man / Down to a sunless sea ... A savage place! As holy and enchanted / As e'er beneath a waning moon was haunted / By woman wailing for her demon-lover!"

Dr. Beltrán was disturbed by my silence, I saw, when again our gazes met. He said he had heard that I had done some writing and suggested that I continue with it.

"And I'll take a moment to fill this prescription." He made notes on a pad. "It will settle your nerves."

After he left the room I was tempted to flee. The pale green light from the lamps was very uncomfortable. It made me think that the room was a part of a harem and that I was a sultan's concubine, waiting for the master's return. The lamps cast a sickly glow onto a shelf behind the desk where there were more shrunken heads with long hair and a large green flask filled with murky objects.

I leaped to my feet and pulled back the purple curtains. The sun was shining on the sea, smoldering like a banked fire on the copper roof of my tower. But as I stood there, suddenly happy, I heard from afar, then closer, the sound of carriage wheels, the pounding of hoofs on the road that led down from the mines, then voices outside in the village street.

After a few moments Dr. Beltrán came back. He now wore a white jacket. It was spattered with blood.

"Men from Mine Number Three," he said. I might have saved one if I'd had him sooner. Minutes, seconds count in this business. They counted just now."

81

He was angry, pacing to the window as he spoke and back again to face me. "Can't you do something about this situation?"

"What?"

"See that we have an ambulance at each of the shafts, anything, even a truck, to get the injured here promptly. The carriage takes forever."

My father had never permitted automobiles or motorcycles or airplanes on Isla del Oro — anything that caused smoke and noise and, above all, reminded him of the *gringo* world outside. I was silent. I felt his hand on my shoulder. I heard his voice.

"Today," Dr. Beltrán said, "the horse-drawn carriage cost a man his life."

"You might talk to Villaverde. Explain everything to him," I said, knowing full well that Villaverde, as quickly as my father, would refuse the request.

Dr. Beltrán bowed and handed me a package of sleeping potion, which I saw was stained with blood. "Be sure and take this," he said. "It will ease your mind. And come back tomorrow. We've made a beginning."

11.

The Warning Beam

BACK IN THE TOWER, I TOSSED THE PACKAGE through the window and the wind sent it hurtling out into the air, down to the beach below. After a time, as I watched the waves gather it in, there was a loud knock at the door. Thinking that Doña Catalina had followed me, anxious to learn how I had fared with Dr. Beltrán, I didn't answer. The knock was repeated, louder this time, and Father Martínez made himself known.

"I was on the terrace," he said, closing the door behind him, "sitting there occupied with my breviary, when this object came sailing by close to my head. It nearly brained me. I looked up to learn where it had come from and spied you standing at the window. She is sending a signal, I thought. She wants to have a talk. Perhaps she wishes to explain why she was not present at our services for two days running. So, obediently, here I am. Only next time please don't throw rocks."

"A potion," I said. "From Dr. Beltrán. To make me sleep."

"I noticed that your lights were burning late last night and the night before. Later than usual. Is anything wrong, my child?"

"Everything," I said.

"Well, let's start and go down the list, one by one." He was trying to be lighthearted, but his furrowed brow belied him. "First off, there's Porfirio. What about this young man? You don't seem to like him. And yet you're engaged to marry him. I am puzzled about this."

"And so am I."

"He's dashing, even with the eyepatch and cane. And I don't think he's a fortune hunter, though his mother is. He appears to be interested only in the mines."

"More than he is in me."

"A serious young man."

"And arrogant," I added. "Selfish and arrogant."

Father Martínez bit on his thumbnail for a moment. "What about Señor Villaverde? You don't get along, the two of you."

He was about to bring up the subject of Doña Catalina, putting off the bad moment as long as he could. He knew why my lights burned late, why I missed meals, why I didn't come to chapel for any of the services.

He chewed on his thumbnail again. I came to his

84

rescue. "I am just back from Dr. Beltrán's office. We talked about the scene in the library. No doubt you have heard."

Father Martínez started to say that he hadn't heard, then changed his mind and said, "A little. You saw a cigar in the ashtray, smelled cigar smoke, and saw the imprint of your father's body in the chair. It's all natural. You are terribly upset about your father. Remember that he had a powerful influence on your life. He laid down the rules you lived by. He told you what to do, almost hour by hour, and you obeyed. From fear? From love? For some other reason? Who knows?"

Father Martínez crossed himself. "You can't expect to free yourself from him in a day or a week. It may take a year. At least you don't think that your father is majestically watching Isla del Oro and all its inhabitants from some golden tower. Señor Villaverde does, I am certain. But you . . ."

The priest's voice had changed. He had grown impatient. I decided not to mention the caskets, but he brought them up in the next breath.

"You were troubled when you went to the basement and found the caskets missing. There was nothing mysterious about this. Señor Villaverde moved them back to the crypt in broad daylight. He told me that he did so because that's where the caskets belong. It is where Don Enrique *wishes* them to be."

"*Wishes?*"

"Yes, not where he *wished* them to be when he was alive, but where he *wishes* them to be. Now, at this very moment. Strange!"

85

"Strange," I said, but by *strange* I did not mean Villaverde's thoughts and actions. It was my own wrong belief that there was something mysterious about the caskets being moved from the basement to the crypt. I should have known why they were moved.

Suddenly a scene from *The Woman in White* forced itself upon me. I saw the schoolhouse in the village of Limmeridge, as Wilkie Collins had described it — the schoolmaster seated at his high desk haranguing the students cowering in front of him, all but one who sat alone in a corner. I heard the schoolmaster say, "Mind what I tell you. If I hear another word spoken about ghosts in this school, it will be the worse for all of you. There are no such things as ghosts. And, therefore, anyone who believes in ghosts believes in what can't possibly be . . ."

And I heard him ask the pupil who sat in the corner when the ghost had been seen.

"At the gloaming," was the reply.

"In the twilight. And what was it like?"

"All in white. As a ghost should be," came the answer.

"I mean to cane the ghost out of the school," the schoolmaster said, "and out of you also."

Father Martínez was acting like the schoolmaster. He was doing his best to cane the ghosts out of me, but he was wasting his time. I didn't believe in ghosts — the ghost the pupil saw all in white turned out to be a strolling woman in a white dress. And yet it seemed there must be a presence abroad in the castle — perhaps spectral, perhaps supernatural — that I could not account for. Either that or, God forbid, my mind had become clouded. As Doña Catalina and Doña Octavia thought. As Father Martínez seemed to fear.

He cleared his throat, quit chewing on his thumb. "You have responsibilities," he said. "Things you need to do while there's still time. Señor Villaverde will stop everything the day he becomes your guardian. And that day can't be far off — a month at the most. As you know — or do you? — he has ordered work stopped on all the wiring above the first floor. He is trying to get a court order to halt work on the lighthouse the Coast Guard is erecting on Punta del Sur. He has suspended for the time being the electric wiring in the mines."

Father Martínez paused to take a breath. "You can do something about all these things, if you see fit. For myself, I would like electricity, so I won't have to crank the telescope up and down by hand. I'd think that you would like to have light in your tower to read by, and not candles. And you might put away the old classics that you've worn out and purchase some new books."

He wanted me to run downstairs, put the electricians to work, talk to the Coast Guard, have an interview with the mine superintendent, make a tour of the mines. And order a shipload of books. I said nothing and didn't move.

"There are things you can't do," Father Martínez went on, keeping his eyes on me. "Like stopping Villaverde from being a guardian. But there are tasks you *can* do instead of wasting your time mooning about ghosts, imagining things that don't exist, reading messages that were never written, hearing commands that no one ever gave, words that were never spoken."

I met his challenging gaze. I didn't flinch.

"You might also attend services again," he said. "There'll be one this evening as usual, held this time especially for those who have strayed into the thorny paths."

I didn't attend his service at dusk, nor did I appear for dinner.

A dry *santana* had blown since early dawn, but now the wind had died away, the dust had settled, and the chain of lights along the mainland coast shone clear beneath a mottled sky. In the harbor men were working on the wharf under the white beam of a seachlight, carrying aboard the *Infanta*'s weekly cargo of gold.

Then the gangway was hauled in. With a long blast from her horn, the ship cleared the harbor and sailed through the Narrows. I pictured myself standing on her deck, watching Castillo Santiago fade into the distance, fade until the walls, every tower, and every battlement faded too, and with them all my troubles.

And yet, my gaze fixed upon the vanishing ship, I realized that by fleeing Isla del Oro I could not flee from myself. Wherever I went in this world, I still could not hide. Wherever it was, Lucinda de Cabrillo y Benivides would be there also.

I don't know how long I stood at the window — seconds, minutes, an hour, gripping the ledge with shaking hands — when suddenly there was a voice at the door. It was Doña Catalina.

"I heard a strange sound," she said, "while I was on the stairs. As of someone falling into a pit. Are you well? Shall I call a servant?"

I stood quietly at the window. After a while she went away. The *Infanta* had disappeared. The sea was black save for a long finger that reached out from the lighthouse on Point Firmin, a warning light, now green, now red.

I slept fitfully that night but rose at dawn and went to early service — for the first time in weeks. In his most dramatic tones, Father Martínez preached on a Biblical parable about the dangers of shirked duties. Annoyed to hear this sermon for the second time, I barely listened, and put off the tasks I had planned to undertake at once until a few days later, when Señor Villaverde suddenly brought them to mind.

He said, drawing me aside after dinner, "You're aware that all electrical work has been halted in the castle," he said. "And that I am following out your father's wishes in the matter."

Villaverde had just returned from five days in Los Angeles. In that brief time his manner had changed. There were fewer bows now, no compliments on my dresses, and a confident look about him that led me to believe he had received favorable news about his efforts to establish himself as my guardian.

"Electricity," he went on, "was seen as an abomination by your father. Don Enrique never permitted it to be used anywhere on the island. Even in the smelter. I am sure, *señorita,* that you share his feelings."

I said nothing — I may even have nodded — but the next morning I ordered Captain Orozco to send for the engineers who had installed the generators and to begin wiring the remainder of the castle. In less than a week the machines were working, and a few days later the whole castle was wired. Only the pantheon and crypt were still lit by candles.

During this time I saw Villaverde every evening at dinner. He knew that all the upper floors of the castle had been wired, because the castle shone like a fairyland, every window a glowing jewel in the night. But he said little. And of this, nothing to show that he was waiting for the day when he could order the power turned off and the candles lit once more.

A few nights later a strange thing happened. A storm had blown up from Mexico that day, but now at midnight the sky had suddenly cleared. I was awakened by a strong beam seemingly focused upon my bed, a light that changed from red to green and red again, like the light across the strait at Point Firmin.

I got out of bed and went to the window. The beam was coming from the new lighthouse on Punta del Sur, a mile away, a site that Señor Villaverde had located after he had given up the long fight against the Coast Guard.

I went back to bed, but the light swept across the room — red and green, then red again — through the night. Had Villaverde deliberately contrived to place the lighthouse there on South Point so that its powerful beam would shine in my tower window?

12.

Centurion

THE NEXT EVENING PORFIRIO APPEARED FOR DINNER minus his cane and eyepatch. He no longer looked the swashbuckling pirate about to board a defenseless ship. But he was still the same arrogant young man, strikingly handsome, thin and pale, with a black, defiant gaze that seemed to challenge, if not the whole world, then all within his sight.

From the day he arrived on the island, full of his studies at the university, Porfirio had disagreed with Salvador Zoyo, our superintendent.

Zoyo had worked in the fabulous silver reefs of Zacatecas, both as a miner carrying a pick and as a foreman. On one of his trips to Mexico, my father had met him, was impressed with his knowledge of mining, and brought him back to the island.

Part Spanish and part Nayarit Indian, he possessed the physical features of both — a beak of a nose, tawny skin drawn tight over his cheekbones. In temperament he was a mixture of the haughty Spaniard and the stubborn Nayarit, hard-working and loyal, who never forgot a slight or reprimand.

The two sat at the far end of the table, out of my hearing, but I became aware before dinner was half over that they were disagreeing about something. Porfirio was making gestures with both hands, while Zoyo sat stolidly looking into his plate.

After dinner, when they continued their argument in the music room, I learned that Porfirio was questioning some of the superintendent's practices, especially his neglect of the tailings left after the gold was extracted from the ore.

I heard him say to Zoyo, "From what you tell me, *señor,* you are dumping a fortune into the sea every day." And I heard Zoyo reply, "I give back to the earth its rightful share. We are not *ladrones* here on Isla del Oro, thieves who take from the earth and give back nothing."

These pagan words, fraught with mystical Indian meaning, annoyed Porfirio, the student of modern metallurgy, but he was silent. Villaverde overheard them and spoke up to say that Zoyo was the best mining engineer in the world and should not be bothered by new, half-baked ideas.

Porfirio remained silent until the two men had left. "The old buzzard's using methods thought up two hundred years ago," he said to me. "He's losing millions every year. I have an idea or two that will bring the operation up to date and save us millions."

I was not surprised that he wanted to intrude himself in the mining operation. From the hour he had arrived, by gestures and by word, Porfirio had considered the island his own — half of it, at least.

"Where's the big smelter located? I've seen the small one."

"South of the river."

"How far?"

"A long league. Too far to walk. There's no road, only a trail."

"No road? The gold is carted out on horseback?"

"On burros. A burro train comes from the smelter every afternoon, every day the *Infanta*'s in port."

"Picturesque but unprofitable. One of Zoyo's notions, no doubt?"

"My father's notion. He liked to sit on the terrace and watch the train come down from the hills and wind through the village. The burros wear gold bells around their necks, and they make tinkling sounds as they trot along. My father liked to hear them."

"Every tinkle a thousand dollars," Porfirio said.

"You can ride one of the burros if you go to the smelter," I said. "They're very docile, so you needn't be afraid of being tossed off."

Porfirio didn't care for this remark, but he made light of it and smiled.

"I've never ridden a burro," he said. "And I don't want a docile beast. You must have a horse or two around here somewhere."

"Captain Vega has twenty-five or thirty. His *pistoleros* ride them on patrol."

"Then I'll borrow a horse in the morning. Two, one

for each of us. We'll investigate the smelter and see what can be done to improve operations."

I hadn't ridden a horse in months, and I lacked any desire to take a long ride in the hot sun. But he kept on until I consented to meet him after breakfast the next morning.

Porfirio overslept, I wasted hours trying to slip away from Doña Catalina, so it was noon before we reached the stables. I had sent word to Captain Vega that we were coming and to have horses ready.

Porfirio's mount was a gray with white stockings, a trim little gelding, a fine match for my gray mare. He walked around the horse twice and then turned to Captain Vega.

"A good pony," he said. "But I am not going out to play polo. Do you have something more suited to the trail?"

"This one's on the trail every day," Captain Vega said. "But if you want a larger horse you can have it."

One of his Indians brought out a dappled mare. Porfirio walked around it, examining its mouth and its hooves while Captain Vega waited.

I had seen little of the captain in the past month, and then only by chance. I had invited him to dinner on two occasions, but he had pleaded illness both times. He had put great hopes into the insane scheme of capturing the atomic plant at San Onofre, and when my father died and the scheme collapsed, he was left a silent, vengeful man, whose courtesy toward me barely concealed that in some curious, warped way he blamed me for Don Enrique's death.

Porfirio shook his head. "A woman's horse," he commented. "Is there something with more spirit, more fire? I don't wish to be difficult . . ."

Captain Vega had not met Porfirio before, but he certainly knew that he was on Isla del Oro and had formed some opinion of him. What he thought of Porfirio now showed in his eyes, as he turned them upon me for an instant — a sinister look that always, no matter that I had seen it since I was a child, sent a chill down my back.

"Bring Centurion," he said to the Indian. "Have someone help you. And give me the heavy bit. The Spanish bit with the wheel and the Spanish spurs. And don't stand there gawking."

Centurion was a dangerous young stallion, big and milk white, with a darting eye. He had killed two of the *pistoleros,* but Captain Vega rode the beast to mass on feast days, dressed in his gaucho costume embroidered with silver, with silver bit and bridle and a saddle studded with *conchas.*

"He's headstrong," Vega said. "Use the bit and the rowels freely if he gets crazy."

Porfirio strapped on the spurs and, favoring his ankle, climbed into the saddle. Taking the reins from the Indian, who scurried away from Centurion's heels, he flicked the stallion hard with the heavy spurs and started off with a leap. He made one circuit of the corral holding the reins and a second waving his arms, and came to a rearing halt in front of me, so close that I was flecked with bits of foam.

"*Excelente,*" he shouted. "*Maravilloso!*"

I clapped my hands politely, surprised at his horsemanship, but Captain Vega muttered a word of caution.

"*Cuidado,*" he said. "Centurion's a devil, *señor,* and like the devil he has cunning tricks."

Captain Vega sent us off with a smart salute, a forced smile, and the cold glance that always sent a chill down my back.

Porfirio moved away at a quick *pasotrote* and I followed him down the village street. We passed the hospital, where Dr. Beltrán was sitting under a striped umbrella, having his lunch and reading a book. The book's cover must have been encrusted with semi-precious jewels and small mirrors, for it gave off tiny flashes of light. The doctor waved, then rose when he recognized us and waved again.

"There's something about the man I don't like," Porfirio said. "Why should he stand up and wave? It's obsequious. He reminds me of a teacher I once had named Pasha. Pasha was thin like Beltrán and also a fawner, always bowing and grinning. One day he stabbed his wife and neatly chopped up her body and hid it under the floor. Dug out the stones one by one and buried the neat little pieces. He even bowed and grinned as they hung him up by the neck."

"What did Pasha teach?" I asked.

"Everything — social science, language, poetry."

"And what did you learn?"

"Not to be obsequious. Not to fawn. To be yourself and say what you think."

"Even if it makes you seem arrogant?"

"Yes."

"Even if it hurts people?"

"Yes."

"Even if it lands you in trouble?"

"Trouble is the common lot. The meek share it equally with the strong."

We came to the first of the two smelters, the small one that used mercury to separate gold from the ore, where my father had his shop and worked to discover the lost secret of Damascene steel. After another short ride we passed Mine Number One, the one my grandfather had discovered, whose tunnels ran like tentacles beneath the castle.

After another league of travel, during which Porfirio showed off his remarkable horsemanship by leaving the trail from time to time on forays into the brush, we came to the main smelter.

"Just as I expected," Porfirio said, casting a disapproving eye over the building, which was large but in need of repair. "You'd think Zoyo would take the trouble to at least paint the door."

He tied Centurion at the gate, disappeared into the building, and was back in minutes with the news that Superintendent Zoyo had gone to the village and would not return before nightfall.

"I didn't need to make a tour," he said. "The sluice boxes are made of wood. The machinery is old. The plant is primitive. Something you might have found a hundred years ago."

"That's when it was built," I said. "And yet it has produced millions upon millions in gold."

"In three months' time I can double the production," Porfirio said. "At least ten percent of the gold is being sluiced into the sea. I'll take a few samples at Bahía de Oro and along the way. They'll prove what I am saying."

I reminded him that in less than an hour the sun would set, that we would have trouble getting home in the dark. He dashed into the smelter and came back with a lantern. We took the trail to Bahía de Oro, moving at a quick pace to the jingle of Porfirio's bag of instruments.

13.

Sea of Sludge

THE SMELTER STOOD IN A DESOLATE ARROYO. THE oaks that once surrounded it had died over the years and were now gray stumps. Above the smelter a small stream had been dammed up to form a pond, which fed water into the sluice boxes and washed gold from the rock.

After it left the smelter, the sludge ran down the dry stream bed toward two high cliffs half a mile away. I had never been that far. The cliffs were copper-colored and their outlines together formed a crude Indian's head and feathered headdress. Sometimes when I was ill I saw this Indian warrior in my dreams, mounted on a horse and carrying a spear.

Since the smelter was not working at this hour, the stream bed was dry except for occasional pools around the rocks and stumps. At each of these pools Porfirio took samples of the tailings and stored them away in a bag he had brought along.

The trail was overgrown with cactus and night-shade, and we saw no sign of recent travel. Shortly before dusk we came to the two high cliffs and passed between them, so close that my knees brushed their stony sides. Here the stream disappeared into a sink-hole and then appeared again in a few yards. Beyond lay Bahía de Oro.

In times past it had been a large, oval bay. Through the years tailings had flowed down from the smelter and formed a bar, which had shut off the ocean tides. Since then, the bay had slowly filled with sludge, until now there was no sign that Bahía de Oro had ever been an arm of the sea. It looked more like a vast, treeless desert, a place on the barren moon.

The sun was nearly down as we came to the end of the trail. Here, when the smelter was running, the stream debouched into Bahía de Oro. Porfirio got off Centurion and went to the end of the channel for samples.

As he was putting the last one away, I heard what I thought was a peal of thunder. But the sky was clear from horizon to horizon, and we were too far away to hear any blast from the mines. There was a second thunderous sound. Then the sound became a contin-uous roar, and the ground began to shake.

I was astride my mare, only a few paces from the channel, when an ugly yellow tongue shot up from the sinkhole, hung in the air for a moment, slowly coiled back upon itself, and then became a cresting billow of mud that rushed roaring toward the bay.

I shouted to Porfirio, but he had already seen the

danger. He was running toward me along the dry channel. The billow swept him from his feet, enveloped him, and he sank from view. Then he came up some distance away, just his head showing.

I leaped from the mare and took a quick step toward him. My foot sank into what seemed a bed of quicksand. I pulled away and stood there helplessly, too frightened to move, aware that by the time I rode back to the smelter and found help he would be dead, drowned in the treacherous sludge.

Porfirio raised his arms in an effort to swim. Then he was still. Then I heard his voice. What he said I didn't understand, but Centurion must have heard the sound, for he began to neigh.

Tied to his saddle was a length of rope, a lariat. I untied it and shook out the coils. I had never held a lariat before, though I had seen our *vaqueros* lassoing cattle in the hills. I spread one end and swung it above me, letting out rope as I did so, making a loop.

Porfirio's head, now barely showing above the billows of yellow sludge, was turned away. I threw the loop toward him, but it only went halfway, at least ten feet short of where he was struggling. As I drew the lariat in and coiled it again, I lost sight of him. The sun had set. The failing light gave off a deceptive glow. It looked as if the sheets of sludge were moving toward me, carrying Porfirio with them.

I threw the lariat again. This time a hand reached slowly out of the muck and grasped it. Braced hard against a rock, I pulled with all my strength, but to no avail. Then, suddenly, as Porfirio seemed to be losing his grip, it occurred to me to tie my end of the rope to the mare's saddle, which I did, clumsily yet securely. In this way, a foot at a time, we dragged him to the shore.

Still clutching the bag of samples, Porfirio scrambled to his feet, and by lantern light I helped him as best I could to clean off the worst of the sludge. Sobered by the accident, we rode silently up the canyon.

The smelter was running when we arrived. Superintendent Zoyo stood at the entrance, his bulky figure outlined against the glare of the stamping mill.

He waved and called to us. "*Hola,* my friends!"

Porforio didn't return the greeting. Instead, he rode across the yard to where Zoyo was standing. I heard him say, "As you observe, *señor,* we are still alive. Barely."

The greenish light from the mill was blinding, and I couldn't see Zoyo's face, but he was puzzled. "You are covered with mud. You fell, *señor?* Come and be washed. I feel sorry for you, *señor.*"

Disgruntled, Don Porfirio didn't answer. We left Zoyo standing there in the green light and rode down the trail, I leading the way with the lantern.

"What a stupid way to die," Porfirio said. "Drowned in the muck of your own mines. As the expression goes, I seem to be accident prone."

"That wasn't an accident," I said. "Someone tried to kill us, both of us."

"That's foolish, *muy loco,*" Don Porfirio said, still disgruntled. "I have never known anyone so full of suspicion. You're suspicious of everything and everybody. It must come from living here on the island."

I couldn't answer him. My lips wouldn't move. I began to tremble and couldn't stop.

Porfirio said, "We're safe. That's all that matters." Then, seeing the lantern shake and go out of my hands, he said, "Get hold of yourself now, or we'll find you in the hospital."

He relit the lantern and we rode on along the trail. Castillo Santiago loomed in the distance. Its lights, shining from a hundred windows, should have had a welcoming look, but gave off instead a sinister glow like some poisonous night flower.

The terrace was flooded with light. Standing on the steps were Doña Octavia and the duenna, Doña Catalina.

"I have been waiting hours," Doña Octavia shrieked, clasping Porfirio to her bosom, although she could see that he was covered with mud. "Whatever has happened? Are you hurt?" Then she glanced at me. "And you? Please tell me, I am dying of fright."

Jaws set and eyes glittering, Doña Catalina said, "I shall inform Señor Villaverde about your running away like this. It's scandalous!"

I was silent. What was there to say? If I had thought of something, I could not have said it. Still trembling, I went without dinner and crawled into bed and lay there with my eyes open, staring at the walls. I got up and went to the window and stared at the empty sea. I got back into bed; then, remembering that Father Martínez was holding a class in astronomy, I dressed and went to the tower. As I walked through the door, the big telescope, silent as a pointing finger, was raising itself toward the heavens.

"I've already thanked you," Father Martínez said. "But thank you again. The electric motor's saved my life. I no longer break my back turning a crank every time I open or close the dome. Señor Villaverde is bent on returning us to the days of candlelight, but with your help I will see that he doesn't."

I told him what had happened at Bahía de Oro. I couldn't remember everything, but some of the horror came back to me in jagged pieces. He listened to my stuttering words as if he had heard them before.

"The sluice runs every day," he said, "but never at fixed hours. It's run for years. And before you were born. I am surprised you didn't know this. Bahía de Oro is not safe at any time. And accidents are a common thing at the smelter. A man was killed just a few days ago." He looked at me with the same suspicion I had seen before, when I told him about the library and the crystal caskets and the mysterious letter that had disappeared. "You're not seeing ghosts?" he said sharply. "Not again, are you?"

The accusation and its tone made me angry. "You know that is all past, Father. The ghosts have gone. I've told you so on my knees in the confessional. Not once but twice. Not twice but three times. And now, I tell you again."

"Good," Father Martínez said. "Good. I believe you. Now you can forget Bahía de Oro and lay aside your suspicions." He went on to suggest that I give my time and energy to other, worthier things. "Let Porfirio make his own experiments. That's his business. You have enough to do without getting yourself mixed up with the mines."

In the midst of this advice, his class in astronomy — made up of Castillo Santiago's servants — walked in and took their places on the platform. I was about to sneak out the door when he summoned me to adjust the eyepiece, and said to the class:

"There are swarms of Geminids tonight, but they move too fast for the telescope. You can see these meteors better with your naked eyes. Let's take a look at Jupiter instead. But first let us review the universe."

I had heard this review before and gave my attention to the telescope.

"This small piece of earth we live on," he said, "turns around once every twenty-four hours at a speed of about one thousand miles an hour. And while it turns it also makes a yearly trip around the sun, which is but one small star in an immense constellation, which likewise turns. And this constellation to which we belong is only a small fragment of the great Milky Way, which holds in a tight embrace some five or six billion stars, many of them thousands of times larger than our star, the sun."

Here Father Martínez paused, praying that his students, who included two butlers, two maids, and Panchito, the carriage driver, were following the lecture.

Then he said, "And this great galaxy, the Milky Way, which is our home, which has some six billion stars, is just one — one, mind you — of millions of similar galaxies, all of them moving around some other great center — still unknown to us — and traveling in their astral orbits trillions upon trillions of miles each year."

He left his students to contemplate this picture, went below for a drink of wine to fortify himself against the chill night, and came back and asked me to locate the planet Jupiter.

"We'll look first at Europa, which is one of Jupiter's moons, whose temperature varies between two and three hundred degrees below zero. Yet it is possible, inhospitable as it is, that some form of life persists there."

I located the planet for him and then scrambled down the ladder, thinking that Jupiter's moon, for all of its wild temperatures, must be a more hospitable place than Isla del Oro.

14.

Visitor in the Night

THE *INFANTA* CAME BACK FROM THE MAINLAND THE next afternoon, bringing with her the books I had ordered. I had them carted to the library and, working with Alicia and Mercedes, cleared off a section of shelves that had been filled with my father's books on the Italian condottieri of the fourteenth and fifteenth centuries, and stacked the new ones in their place by title and author.

After dinner I took an armful to the tower, prepared to read the night away. But I soon found that I was too upset to read steadily. I read a few pages of *For Whom the Bell Tolls* and set it aside, then a page from *Tender Is the Night.* I picked up *Death Comes for the Archbishop* and turned to the part where the two priests stop on the lonely road to Mora and find lodging with a murderer and his wife. I reached the place where the wife warns the travelers to leave, that if they don't, they will be dead before morning:

"With her finger she pointed them away, away! — two quick thrusts into the air. Then, with a look of horror beyond anything language could convey, she threw back her head and drew the edge of her palm quickly across her distended throat — and vanished."

At this point, the lights flickered and went out.

I lit candles but didn't try to read again. What I had read was already confused in my mind. I blew out the candles, said my prayers, and on an impulse, as a penance for having scolded Mercedes when she put one of the new books on the wrong shelf, I said fifty Hail Marys.

The sky — what I could see of it — was a dome of toppling clouds. The quarter-moon cast slivers of light through the window, across the marble floor, and touched the foot of my bed.

I must have been asleep for an hour. In any event, soon after *Infanta*'s clock had struck the hour of one, I became aware of a mild discomfort.

I had been dreaming of being chased by a man in a scarlet mask — I never before had seen colors in my dreams — chased along a rocky yellow shore, much like the shore at Bahía de Oro, then across the bay itself, sinking to my knees in sludge, every step I took heavy and painful.

The moon had shifted and the clouds had massed together, but the walls of the room still were bathed in silver light. I made out a shape at the foot of my bed, or thought I did. At first it seemed to be a heavy comforter. The night was chill and sometimes while I was asleep Mercedes, finding the door unlocked, slipped in and left it for me. Then, as I was about to reach down and pull it up, I saw that the comforter had a curious shape and a peculiar color.

I raised my head for a clearer view of the object. I was careful not to move my legs, for something told me that I was in danger. Then I saw that coiled upon my feet lay the deadly bushmaster.

The serpent might have wandered into the tower by way of the secret stairs. Someone could have placed it on the bed. Possibly it was asleep, possibly drugged; I wasn't sure. I could scream for help, but the noise would surely rouse it.

I remembered the curator's description of the bushmaster word for word, as he had sent it to us when the serpent had been loosed upon the beach from the wrecked ship. *"Lachesis muta,"* he wrote, "is a pit viper more than twelve feet in length, marked by black bars and pink shadings. Its aggressive nature, its ability, because of its length, to strike human prey in the throat, and its long fangs supplied with copious venom, make the bushmaster the deadliest snake in the world, deadlier than the king cobra or the mamba. Extreme care in handling the bushmaster is suggested. It may be well to remember, however, that this viper is reluctant to attack unless provoked."

The words *this viper is reluctant to attack unless provoked* rang in my ears. I saw again the scene in the crypt as the bushmaster followed my father down the row of caskets like a faithful dog. Then I saw my father turn, raise his two fists, and shout at me, "Traitoress!" Mistakenly, the serpent believed itself threatened by the angry words and the raised fists. It quickly gathered its coils and sprang, its pink jaws opened wide.

I lay very quiet. It was hours before dawn, before Mercedes would come to the door and knock and bring me a tray of wafers and morning chocolate. When she knocked I would warn her. In the softest of voices, in a whisper, I would tell her about the bushmaster. Before she even came into the room, because the serpent could have moved by then and could be waiting at the door, I would ask her to call the menservants.

Infanta's bell struck the hour of two.

The waves that had been pounding on the rocks below the castle for hours grew quiet as the running tide turned. It was very quiet in the tower, so quiet I could hear the serpent breathing. It made a sound louder than my own frightened breaths, a delicate murmur like a child's innocent slumber. Or was it something I only imagined? Could it be the sound of the waves sliding among the rocks far below?

The moon had withdrawn into the west, but still there was light in the room. The serpent had arranged its coils neatly one upon the other, and upon this pyramid lay its head, flat and broad as my hand. Were its eyes closed? Did serpents close their eyes when they slept? I seemed to recall that they were lidless. The bushmaster could be asleep with its eyes open.

Infanta's bell struck the hour of four. When their echoes had died away, slowly, holding my breath, I withdrew one foot from the burden that pressed upon

110

it. The bushmaster did not move. But as I withdrew the other foot, before I could place it on the floor, the serpent raised its head.

In the last of the moonlight, I saw that it was watching me. If it had been asleep, it was now awake. The effects of any drug had worn off. I lay quiet, scarcely breathing, unsteadily returning the gaze that was fixed upon me.

The bushmaster had seen me before. I had been in the crypt on the fatal night, not five paces away, as the serpent followed my father down the row of caskets, half that distance when it attacked him. Was it possible that the bushmaster recognized me?

After a short while I noticed that the serpent's gaze had grown more intense. Then, though the light was now poor, I believed that I saw more than this. Its head was turning slowly from side to side, as the forked tongue flicked out, in the rhythmic movement of a pendulum. Yes, like the pendulum in Poe's ghastly tale, moving closer and closer toward my exposed heart.

Suddenly I was lying in a Toledo dungeon, sentenced to die by a hooded judge of the Spanish Inquisition. The stone walls were slimy and gave off the smell of decayed fungus. The place was swarming with rats, their red eyes glaring at me as if they were only waiting to make me their prey.

The scene faded, but the serpent's head continued to move back and forth — slowly at times, then faster, as if keeping pace with some strange urge that shifted one way and then another in its dim brain. The forked tongue never ceased to explore the air, which smelled of the sea, now that a dawn breeze came through the window.

I fell into a stupor, not sleep, and awoke to Mercedes' knock. The serpent hadn't changed its position in that time or ceased to move its head. In the gray light of dawn, its amber eyes were fixed upon me with the same quiet intensity.

I had to speak, to answer her knock, or else Mercedes would appear upon the scene unwarned and surely scream. Quietly, with a curious lack of fear, I informed her about the serpent and asked that she not enter the tower until she had called some of the menservants. They came to the doorway, three of them with guns.

The bushmaster did not move from the bed as they stood there. It glanced in their direction, then ignored them and again fixed its amber eyes upon me, so benignly that for a moment I no longer felt a prisoner, as if through the long night it had guarded me from all the pursuing evils.

I sent the men away for a fisherman's net. They returned with a big one and had no trouble gathering up the serpent. They carried it to the window and were about to toss it to the rocks below. Then I remembered an act of Father Junípero Serra, saintly follower of Saint Francis, after he was bitten by a poisonous snake in the wilds of Mexico. As his companion lifted a rock to kill it, Serra had stayed the youth's hand.

"Handle the serpent with care," I said. "Place it in a box marked for the San Francisco zoo, its future home, and see that it is aboard the *Infanta* when she sails north this afternoon."

The hall was crowded with onlookers during the encounter — Doña Catalina and Doña Octavia and all the servants. Everyone except Father Martínez, who was conducting mass, and Don Porfirio, who was asleep exhausted, his mother said.

Dr. Beltrán came in as soon as the serpent had been carried away. He closed the door behind him, took my pulse, shook his head, gave me two green pills with a glass of water, and ordered me to stay in bed.

"You have a strong heart, *señorita*, but it's on a roller coaster at this moment — up and down, up and down. Perhaps we should discuss your experience." His eyes, heavy-lidded and sleepy, regarded me gently. "How do you feel?"

"Shaky."

"Too shaky to talk?"

"I wonder."

He sat beside the bed and asked me questions, which I answered slowly, feeling that I was not talking about myself but someone else.

"You were asleep," he said, "and awakened to find the snake lying at your feet?"

"On my feet."

"Pardon — *on* your feet. You heard no noises? Nothing?"

"Nothing."

"The snake could not have crawled through the window? Nor could it have been placed there?"

"It is five stories from the ground to this tower."

113

"What's below the tower?"

"A hallway. Stairs leading to a lower floor. But there are no windows on either of the floors."

"I know that the snake killed your father," Dr. Beltrán said. "I also know that it wanders around in the crypt. That Señor Villaverde has it fed and taken care of by one of the servants."

"By Alicia."

"When did you last see it?"

"Three days ago, in the crypt. It lives there. There's a crack in the floor, and it goes and comes as it pleases."

"A member of the household, so to speak?" Dr. Beltrán lowered his voice. "I have heard about the accident at Bahía de Oro. Now this. Much of what has happened you may have imagined, but not the serpent. It was there on your bed last night. It was there this morning. It has just been taken away. I saw it."

He paused to arrange his gown, which had parted at the knees, exposing a pair of black trousers. "You seem to believe that someone planted the snake on your bed. That it did not get there by itself. You certainly don't have an enemy among the servants?"

"There are some who dislike me, but I doubt any of them would go that far."

"How do you and this Captain Vega make out?"

"I employ him to guard the island from intruders."

"Then it wouldn't be in his interest to harm you."

"Captain Orozco I also employ. Father Martínez and I are friends."

"That leaves the superintendent of mines, Zoyo,

who is likewise an employee, and Señor Villaverde, who is not."

"Zoyo was always loyal to my father. Villaverde was my father's valet, and as far as I am concerned he is still a valet."

"Now. But when he becomes your guardian?"

"Señor Villaverde's fortunes, even more than those of the others, are bound up with mine. Without me, he has nothing to guard."

A tremor shook the room. It came from a blast beneath the castle, at the tunnel in Mine Number One. I was accustomed to these tremors — there were usually two or three every day — and thought nothing about them, but for some reason this one started my blood racing.

Dr. Beltrán was watching. I wondered if he could hear the wild beating of my heart. He must have heard it, for he gave me another pill, a brown, bitter one this time, which put me fast asleep. After long, dreamless hours, I was awakened by the *Infanta*'s horn.

I rose and went to the window. The ship was passing the Narrows, turning north into the open sea. At this moment, as the ship disappeared carrying away the serpent — God's beautiful creature doomed to crawl upon the earth, despised by everyone — my mind cleared at last.

Suddenly I glimpsed the truth. Someone on the island, beginning with the scene in the library, then the cryptic letter, and now the bushmaster, sought to drive me mad.

15.

Underground

DON PORFIRIO, WHO HAD SLEPT SOUNDLY THROUGH
my encounter and apparently hadn't heard about it,
was jubilant when I met him at breakfast the next
morning, so jubilant that I decided to say nothing
about the serpent.

"I've worked all night on the samples I took at
Bahía de Oro," he said, "and as I predicted, the sludge
that Zoyo sluices off into the bay contains a high per-
centage of gold."

Nothing interested me less than the idea of digging
up a bay full of sludge, but loath to dampen his spirits, I listened for most of an hour while, with scarcely
a pause, he described his plans.

"First," he said, ordering the butler to take away
the plate of food he hadn't touched, "let's talk about
Mine Number One. I looked at the books yesterday — incidentally, they're badly kept. We're being
robbed blind by somebody, probably Zoyo. Produc-

116

tion slumped badly last year. Worse, it's been slumping for several years. There are reasons for the slump, suspicious ones, but I have no authority to investigate them. The authority is yours, until the day Señor Villaverde takes over the island and your affairs. At that moment it will be too late to discover what's wrong. Who is cheating us out of our millions and how it's being done."

Porfirio's untouched food had been taken away, but he had kept his knife and was now making designs on the tablecloth — a pickax, a shovel, a lump of ore. Suddenly he informed me that he had arranged for us to visit mine *Numero Uno.*

"Tomorrow," he said.

"For what reason?"

"I want Zoyo to see that you stand behind me in whatever I am forced to do."

"I'll write him an order."

"He doesn't read."

"Then I'll speak to him."

"Zoyo doesn't listen. Indians don't, I have found. They nod and smile and don't listen. Words bounce off their stubborn heads like rain off the roof. Tomorrow we visit the mine."

"The miners, and there are several hundred down there, won't like it," I said. "They're very superstitious. They're like sailors in the old days who thought it bad luck to see a woman on board a ship. Our miners think it bad luck for a woman to be seen in the mines."

"Who told you this folk tale?"

"My father. It was always his answer when I asked him if I could go into the mines."

"I am glad to know that you're not afraid of mines, like most women. My mother, for instance, wouldn't go down for all the tea in Timbuktu."

"I've been curious about the mines since I was a child."

"Be ready after lunch tomorrow."

"I haven't anything to wear in a mine."

"Wear a party dress. Your prettiest. The miners will like that. And bring the duenna. We'll lose her in one of the tunnels. Ha, ha."

Mine Number One was within walking distance, but Porfirio, in love with Centurion after the ride to Bahía de Oro, asked Captain Vega for the beast, so we rode to the mine *a pillon,* I riding sidesaddle behind him in the true Spanish mode, on a comfortable pillow, a hand on his shoulder.

"Someday," Porfirio said, "after we're married, we'll go to Seville and ride in the grand fiesta with people pelting us with flowers. My lovely bride and my beautiful horse will be the center of all eyes."

It was the first word in over a month about marriage. He always included himself whenever he mentioned the mines — *"our* mines," "who is cheating *us* out of *our* millions," and so forth. But seldom a word about marriage. The word gave me an odd feeling.

Numero Uno was waiting for us. Spanish flags decorated the shaft entrance. A delegation of five miners, headed by Superintendent Zoyo, welcomed us, while a band of girls and boys sang an Indian song in shrill little voices, which were mostly drowned out by the noises that came floating up the shaft.

Before electricity was brought in, the shaft had been lit by lanterns hung down its full length, some two hundred feet. Now a string of electric bulbs wound to the bottom. At the time the lights were brought in, the government had ordered us to install elevators, both to lift the ore to the surface and transport the miners back and forth to work.

This was put off, not because of the expense but because Villaverde said it was something my father had fought against over the years, by hook and crook had prevented, and still would fight against were he alive.

Rung by rung Porfirio and I let ourselves down the ladder. It went straight down for a dozen rungs, then slanted off at an angle to the bottom of the shaft, some two hundred steps below. The rungs were slippery, polished smooth by the passage of thousands of feet. I held my breath most of the way. When I reached the bottom and looked back, the sky had disappeared, and all I could see above me was a string of feeble lights trailing upward in the gloom.

Superintendent Zoyo had gone down a few minutes before us, carrying a caged canary to make certain that the air we were about to breathe was not poisonous — a precaution staged for effect, because the room where we now found ourselves was crowded with miners, all alive and breathing.

Small, bronzed men, their somber eyes glittering in the light of the lamps fastened to their iron hats, they had been waiting for us to descend. I greeted them with a *"buenas tardes,"* but they didn't return the greeting.

"Arriba!" Zoyo shouted. "Do not stand there staring until your eyes drop out. *Vámanos.*"

One by one, the miners started up the ladder, each with a basket of ore strapped to his back. They sang softly to themselves — it was more of a lament than a song — and when the last one reached the surface, a second line of men came out of a tunnel and went up the ladder. Then the two lines descended in silence, carrying their empty baskets, while a third line waited with full baskets.

"Two thousand years ago, the Romans mined gold in this crude way," Porfirio said to me. "Can you imagine it in this day and age? Here's where some of our millions go. Here and Bahía de Oro."

Out of the darkness came the voice of Señor Villaverde. He stood at an opening not three strides away. Snapping on his torch, he shone it in our faces, first into mine, then Porfirio's.

"The Romans," he said, "were artists, men of refinement and taste. They believed that such a princely metal as gold should not be wrenched from the earth, treated like garbage, but removed from the earth by friendly hands and carried away on friendly backs. And as the great Romans believed, so believed Don Enrique de Cabrillo y Benivides, a man in the Roman mold. And so do I and Salvador Zoyo."

"Wasteful," Porfirio said. "How many work in the mine?"

120

"Zoyo," Villaverde shouted, "how many Indians in the mine?"

"Three hundred and forty," came the answer.

"How many pounds does each one carry at a time?" Porfirio asked.

"Sixty pounds," Zoyo called back.

"How many hours do they work?" Porfirio asked.

"Fifty hours and much time over fifty hours," Zoyo said.

"How much are they paid?"

"As the law permits," Villaverde said.

"What does the law permit?" Porfirio asked.

"Three dollars and thirty-five cents an hour," said Villaverde.

Zoyo was flicking his torch on and off, pointing it at our feet, as if he were shooting a pistol.

"Superintendent Zoyo," Porfirio said, "would you quit aiming your light at us, and when you do stop will you be so kind as to tell me where all this money goes? The Indians don't receive it. I have asked a dozen in the last week and they all say they are getting three dollars and thirty-five cents a day, not an hour."

Zoyo was silent.

"There are certain expenses," Villaverde said. "Lodging. Transportation back and forth to Mexico. Hospitals."

"Many things," Zoyo said, recovering himself. *"Muchas cosas."*

Truthfully, I must say that I thought little about the mines. My childhood interest had long since evaporated. I knew that gold bars poured out of the smelters, were carried on donkey back to the wharf and onto the *Infanta,* which sailed north every week to San Francisco. I saw our miners strolling in the village street on feast days, dressed in their bright serapes. I saw their wives and children at mass. But I had no idea of what went on here in the bowels of the earth — that before the ore ever went to the smelters, before the bars ever poured forth in a golden stream, half-naked men clawed it out of hard stone and carried it on their backs up the two hundred steps of a swaying ladder.

Villaverde said, "You do not like this operation, *señor.* It is too old-fashioned for you. You like lots of big, clanking machinery."

"I like efficiency," Porfirio said.

Villaverde pointed toward a tunnel where a few bulbs struggled with the darkness. Miners' lamps were moving about, giving off sparks of light, and I heard the sound of picks striking stone.

"We work five tunnels," Villaverde said. "They are all mined the same way — by hand tools and dynamite. You will see no machinery. Perhaps you wish to go no farther with your inspection."

"I wish to see the work in one of the tunnels. One is enough, since all five are alike," Porfirio said. Then he turned to me. "You've seen enough, Lucinda, for your first visit. The rest is dangerous."

"Dangerous," said Villaverde, "and the miners work naked because of the heat."

The room was stifling hot and airless. Water clung to the ceiling and splashed at my feet and ran off into

122

a gutter. Wisps of black smoke drifted around me. Through one of the walls I could hear the pounding of the sea.

A line of miners had formed at the mouth of a tunnel, and Zoyo sent them on their way with a shout. "I keep them moving," he said. "These Indians get lazy if you let them stand around too much."

As the last man — a stout fellow carrying a heavier load than the others — disappeared up the dark well, Zoyo escorted me to the ladder and saw that I had a firm hold and that my right foot was set upon the first rung.

"It is unlucky," he explained, "if you start climbing with the left foot. It is bad to do this, *señorita.*"

My legs and arms were still shaking from the trip down, so I gritted my teeth and held my breath. Unable to think of a saint who watched over those who climbed ladders, I asked for help from merciful Mary.

I had climbed about half the distance to the surface and could see the faintest glimmer of daylight when it happened.

16.

Obsession

FIRST, THERE CAME THE MUFFLED THUNDER OF DYNA-mite from one of the galleries below. Its echo faded away into deep silence and the ladder began to sway gently back and forth. Then from above — whether from someone on the surface or one of the miners climbing the ladder, I couldn't tell — came a horrible scream.

A rock struck my forehead. Then a shower of rocks fell around me. I heard the awful scream again, this time drawn out into a wail of terror. The wail ceased. Suddenly the light above me was shut off, and in that moment of darkness an object, a man who reached out to grasp me, hurtled past and was gone.

"Hold on," someone called. "Hold on and take the rope we're letting down. Two rungs are broken above you, but there is no danger. Be calm. The rope is coming."

In the dim light, the rope looked like a writhing

serpent, but I grasped it with both hands. I clung to it for dear life and, bumping against the slippery walls, was hauled slowly past the missing rungs to the surface. I clambered up from my knees. The daylight was blinding, but I recognized Dr. Beltrán striding toward me. I didn't faint in his arms, although I felt like it. Giddily, I remembered that I had put my right foot out when I started up the ladder.

"I feared something might happen," the doctor said. "It's no place for a woman. You're fortunate — a whole basket of ore fell on you, and it's a wonder that the miner didn't knock you off the ladder."

Porfirio, Zoyo, and Villaverde came out of the mine, and Señor Villaverde was solicitous about a cut on my forehead. Then he turned to Zoyo.

"This is the third man you have killed in as many weeks," he shouted, throwing up his arms in a threatening gesture.

"The ladder is very old," Zoyo said calmly. "We make steps for the ladder but it falls apart, *señor.*"

"Perhaps you should build a new ladder," Villaverde said. "Every rung new and of the hardest wood."

"Of ironwood," Superintendent Zoyo said.

A silent ring of men had gathered at the shaft. They held their empty baskets and waited for the rungs to be replaced so they could descend again. Zoyo walked to the shaft and strung a rope across the opening. He told the men to take themselves off to Mine Number Three. The men put the baskets on their backs, but as they started down the hill I decided to stop them.

It was not a sudden decision. I had thought of it before. But I would never have done anything had I not seen the men working in the heat and stink, had I not seen their faces, had I not nearly lost my life on the ladder, had I not suddenly remembered last Easter day, when the *penitentes* had filed in front of the castle, chanting to wailing flutes, *"Dénos, Señor, buena muerte"* — Give us, Lord, a good death — as though only death could repay them for a hard life.

"Go home," I said. "All the mines — this mine and Mine Number Two and Mine Number Three — are closed."

The men stared at me. There was not a sound among them. Villaverde said something to Zoyo. The miners didn't move.

"Go," I shouted. *"Vayan!"*

The men began to file down the hill. Before they had gone far, they stopped and glanced back, not at me, but at Zoyo.

"It's a bad idea, shutting down all the mines," Porfirio whispered to me. "Even this one. Why not repair the ladder and keep the mine open until we can install an elevator? Who knows how long that's going to take? There are over two thousand men working in the three mines. They all have to be paid. Nothing will be coming in. Not a cent."

The miners still stood in the road, looking back, clutching their empty baskets. They seemed puzzled by what had happened, frightened at what might happen next. They were waiting for a sign from Zoyo, *el Hermano Mayor,* the Great Brother of *los Her-*

manos de Luz, the Brothers of Light, as the *penitentes* called themselves.

Villaverde said, "I am afraid you don't understand what you are doing." A wild look in his eyes betrayed his gentle tone.

"It's done," I said. "This mine is closed. The other mines also."

Villaverde's wild look suddenly vanished. He was now gazing upon me with the same patient understanding I had seen in everyone who feared for my sanity.

"I share your fright at this horrible accident," he said. "You have a tender heart, Miss Lucinda. But your order is a needless waste. I hope you will find the wisdom to cancel it."

"If I do, *señor,* I'll send word to Superintendent Zoyo."

At his name Zoyo glanced at the miners and then at me. "They do not understand," he said.

"But you understand, sir. Explain to them why I am sending them home. And tell them that they will receive their wages. Only this time they will receive *all* of their wages. Not what is left over after most has been taken out."

I refrained from accusing him of theft, although I believed what Porfirio had said to him below in the mine — that for years he had systematically robbed the miners.

The men were still waiting for a sign from Salvador Zoyo, Great Brother, *Hermano Mayor.* He stood shading his eyes against the hot sun, glancing at Vil-

127

laverde, then at me, then at the men, weighing us against each other, trying to decide what would profit him the most.

I said, "*Señor,* you are in charge of the mines. But I am the owner of the mines. The mines are closed until the day they're safe. Also, tell your men about the wages. And see that they receive them."

Zoyo hesitated. He was wearing a broad-brimmed sombrero, which he pushed back on his brow. He stood looking at the ground. He took his sombrero off, made a curt bow, and without a word went down the hill toward the village, his men following him. Villaverde watched in silence.

Dr. Beltrán said that I must come to the hospital and have my forehead sewn up. "It needs eight or nine stitches. Otherwise, you'll have a scar."

"I've had stitches before, when I was a child, and I don't like them," I said.

"Also, there's a good chance of infection," he went on, not hearing me. "Mines are full of strange germs."

I argued and lost, was sewn up, and received a patch on my brow. Porfirio and I started back to the castle, no longer the gay young couple riding *a pillon.* I rode astride now, shaken and dizzy, holding onto his broad shoulders.

Fortunately, Doña Catalina was not on the terrace to greet us. Porfirio patted Centurion on the flank and handed him over to the groom.

"Why are you so upset?" he said sharply as we walked inside. "What happened in the mine — the broken rungs — was surely an accident. I hear that happens every week. The ladder's terribly old."

"How many accidents does it take to convince you that someone is trying to harm me? Both of us. First there was Bahía de Oro. Then the bushmaster. Now the ladder."

Porfirio was already looking off into space, thinking of something else.

"Perhaps it's wise, after all, to have the mines shut down," he said. "I'll have a much better chance to inspect them without getting myself blown up. Zoyo is working veins in Mine Number One that must be fifty years old. From the little I saw today, I would say he's only scratched the surface. There's a vein of pure gold at least three feet wide that runs for half a mile or more. It's never been touched. It won't wear out in our lifetimes. Or the lifetimes of our children."

What children, I was tempted to ask.

Scarcely a word had been said about our coming marriage. Since his arrival on Isla del Oro, Porfirio's one interest had been gold. He spent most of his time drawing up complicated plans. He talked about gold at the dinner table. He was obsessed with gold.

I understood his obsession. After all, he had studied mining for years at the university. It was a boyhood dream and his chosen work. From the first night we had met, he had displayed very little interest in my wealth or in what gold meant as a possession or even as power. To him the mines were romance, adventure, life itself. Also efficiency and rules.

Something else suddenly struck me.

Our engagement had been arranged and sealed by

our parents. For years I had accepted it as an unbreakable bond. But now, as I listened to Porfirio talk about the mines, thinking of the endless talk I had already heard from him on this subject, and the talk I would be forced to listen to in years to come, I was seized with doubt. I had freed myself from my father's cold obsession. Had I traded it for another obsession, more human but just as cold?

17.

A Guest in the Tower

BEFORE DAYLIGHT THREE DAYS LATER, DON POR-
firio went into Mine Number One and began to survey the lode he had seen with Villaverde and Superintendent Zoyo. Against my advice, he collected a
gang of *dinamiteros* and made tests.

The new lode, directly beneath the castle, opened
into an abandoned tunnel connected to the crypt.
Over my objections to Porfirio, explosions echoed and
reechoed in the tower. Real mining would begin in a
month. Then the noise would go on night and day, so
I decided to move into the east tower, which was a
distance from the blasting. My plans were interrupted
by Dr. Beltrán.

After a week I went to see him about the stitches in
my forehead. Much gentler than Dr. Wolfe, he sat me
down and severed one of the black threads with an
instrument that looked like a pen but had a sharp little knife at the end. He pulled out the thread with

tweezers and placed it carefully on a gauze pad the nurse held out.

"Upon reflection," he said, "I am further convinced that your life is not in jeopardy. When you were here the first time, a man was brought in from Mine Number One. He died. Two have died there since then. Accidents like those that happened to you and Don Porfirio are common. It's only the bushmaster affair that needs to be explained. Does anyone have a key to your door?"

"Mercedes."

"Others?"

"Possibly."

"Was the door locked that night?"

"No."

"Then someone could come in while you were downstairs and hide the serpent in the tower."

"It's huge. There's nowhere it could be hidden and not be seen."

Dr. Beltrán put the next stitch beside the first one. "You've told me about a passage that leads up from below. From the crypt. The serpent might have crawled along this passage and coiled itself on your bed."

"Why?"

"You have known it for a long time. It killed your father, whom you sometimes hated. From whom you often tried to free yourself. Perhaps the serpent considered itself a friend, a deliverer."

"I've heard of people who have tamed Bengal

tigers, but not of any who have tamed deadly serpents."

"It requires magical powers," Dr. Beltrán said. "And you may have these powers." He regarded me for a moment with his heavy-lidded eyes.

"Someone came from the crypt," I said, "while I was asleep. Either by the stairway or by the passage. And placed the serpent on my bed."

"You're certain?"

"Certain," I said, beginning to tremble.

The Mudéjar eyes searched my face. "To me your fears are unfounded, Miss Lucinda, but to you they're terribly real. Would it be convenient if I moved into the castle? Would you feel safer for my being there?"

"You are welcome, Dr. Beltrán," I managed to say, stuttering. "But what will that do, sir?"

"My presence, the mere fact of my being there, will serve as a warning to any who seek to harm you. If such fools there could possibly be."

He snipped out three more black threads and placed them beside the others. The nurse asked me if it hurt. I shrugged, though each one of the stitches had felt like a small firecracker exploding in my head.

"When do you wish to move?" I said.

"At once. And if it's convenient, I prefer to be in one of the towers. There are four of them, I understand, and two are unoccupied."

"You may have the east tower," I said, beginning to wonder what Doña Catalina and Doña Octavia and

Don Porfirio — what everyone would think. "It's quieter than the others and has a fine view of the mainland coast as far as Mexico."

"It's the closest tower to yours?"

"Yes."

"Excellent! I am more interested in being nearby than in a view of Mexico."

He took out the last of the stitches, put it beside the other eight in a neat little row, and asked the nurse for a mirror.

"You have a scar, but it's not catastrophic," he said.

"I have a lot of scars. One more doesn't make any difference," I said bravely.

But it did. I only glanced at the mirror, not into it, and in a businesslike voice told Dr. Beltrán that I would send servants to move him at once.

When I got back to the castle, I ran for a mirror. Just inside the main lobby, between the grotto and the great courtyard, a whole wall was covered with mirrors, a huge one in the center and smaller ones ranged on both sides. Each gave back a slightly different image. The image in the big mirror — I suppose because it had been made in Venice centuries before and had become a little cloudy — was the most flattering. I chose it.

I was encouraged to find the scar barely visible, no matter which way I moved. Emboldened, I was trying one of the smaller, less cloudy mirrors when Doña Catalina came up behind me. I felt her presence before I saw her.

"I never pass a mirror without gazing at myself," I

said, trying to make conversation. "How does it look?"

"What?" she said, taken by surprise.

"The scar, how does it look?"

She turned my head toward the sunlight that shone in from the door to the great courtyard. "It isn't bad at all," she said. "Of course, you can always wear your hair in a different way. A bang will cover it nicely."

"I don't like bangs."

"Then it will show a bit. But scars are interesting. People will ask you about it and you can make up a wonderful story, for you have a lively imagination. I was fascinated with your description of the imbroglio at Bahía de Oro. And your séance with the serpent. I haven't heard *your* account of the accident at the mine. It should be exciting, too."

Doña Catalina wore a dress with a high neck that was piped with pink net ruching. It seemed to be choking her.

"Dr. Beltrán is moving into the castle," I said without warning, just to shock her.

My duenna's face never changed. Nothing except her breathing. That stopped for a while.

"When does this event take place?" she said.

"Soon."

"He is moving into the castle? Where in the castle?"

"The east tower."

Doña Catalina gasped. "But that's down the passageway from you. How will it look? The servants will surely talk. What will people think? What will your fiancé, Porfirio, think?"

"I haven't the least idea."

She drew herself up. "And what will they think of me, Doña Catalina de Portago, permitting such a scandalous . . ."

"They'll think you're an evil influence. That you've corrupted me. They'll throw stones at you."

I smiled. It induced the duenna to smile also, and to make an unusual suggestion.

"I have been thinking," she said, "that after Easter sometime, perhaps in May, we should have an evening recital."

I was surprised and pleased at this shift in her dour attitude. "A wonderful idea," I said quickly. "You play the lute beautifully. Porfirio has a fine tenor voice. Maybe Dr. Beltrán has a voice, too. We'll have a chorus. The servants always sing at Easter and Christmastime, trooping around the halls, trilling like little birds. How exciting! I'm glad you thought of it."

"So am I," the duenna said, color stealing into her sallow cheeks. "Do you think it would be best to have it in June when all the flowers are out?"

I thought for several moments. "I have a better time. Let's celebrate the day Juan Rodriguez Cabrillo first sighted the coast of California. That was a Sunday, the second of July, in the year fifteen hundred and forty-two."

"We should start practicing soon, so everything will be perfect," Doña Catalina said. "In a week or so, perhaps, after Dr. Beltrán is settled."

"Wonderful," I said.

18.

The Phantom Horse

IT TOOK ALL NEXT DAY FOR THE SERVANTS TO MOVE Dr. Beltrán's things — crates of ivory taborets, swords, scimitars, brass shields, lamps of all shapes and sizes, green bottles filled with odd objects, velvet curtains, Oriental rugs, and his collection of shrunken heads with streaming black hair, just to mention things he had never unpacked.

Porfirio learned of Dr. Beltrán's change of residence that night at dinner, a dinner I gave after Lent, to which I had invited all of the island's dignitaries, their wives, and those of their children who were old enough to sit at table and be seen but not heard. I planned the dinner as a festive occasion, yet beyond this it was meant as a notice to my friends and a challenge to my enemies that Lucinda de Cabrillo y Benivides was the mistress of Isla del Oro, now and in the future.

The first wine had just been served when Dr. Beltrán proposed a toast to Castillo Santiago. I remember all of what he said, especially his flowery concluding words.

"Tonight from my lofty tower at sunset, when velvet shadows were creeping out of the west," the doctor intoned in his beautiful Spanish, which also invoked a longing to taste the forbidden mysteries of Araby, "the sea was like Hector's golden shield, shining too brightly for human eyes to bear. Then the dark came and the golden sea disappeared and the mainland lights shimmered like the jewels at the wedding feast of mighty Belshazzar, king of Babylon."

I was watching Porfirio's face at the moment he first realized that Dr. Beltrán had moved into the castle. He turned pale, deathly pale. His lips parted in what began as a smile and ended in an awkward grin. When he glanced at me, I expected to see sparks leap forth, but his eyes were stony cold.

After dinner, while the men lingered over their brandy, I shepherded the wives and children into the Great Hall. I left them there, happily to eat fancy ices and listen to a marimba band, and the duenna and I went off to the music room to practice for our recital. Doña Octavia trailed along. Before I sat down at the harpsichord, she informed me that Don Porfirio had gone to the mine on business.

"He's working so hard," she said. "And getting so thin it worries me. Alas, when he puts his heart on something, he can't eat or sleep until it is done. I wish he would listen to me. Perhaps a word from you will reach him. You'll try, my dear, won't you?"

"I've tried already. My attempts only served to spur him on."

"You must try again. It is a difficult time for the three of us." She paused to straighten a ribbon I wore at my neck.

I hoped that Doña Octavia had not heard Beltrán — after all, she rarely listened to other people's talk — and hadn't realized that he had moved into the castle, or else knew and thought nothing of it.

"I can understand why you look to Dr. Beltrán for counsel," she said as I sat down at the harpsichord. "He is such a friendly young man."

The duenna sat beside me and we began our practice for the recital. Doña Octavia, turning the pages for us, was quiet until we made our first mistake and stopped. Then she went on about Dr. Beltrán.

"The doctor is very friendly, but he's an Arab, and Arabs are known to be pushy. He could become an awful nuisance."

After a moment or two, while the duenna did something to her lute, Doña Octavia said, "You have a very trusting nature, Lucinda. And you seem to like everyone, no matter what."

For nearly an hour the duenna and I practiced, Doña Octavia turning the pages with her plump little hands. When we finished, she drew me aside.

"It worries me," she said, "that you and Porfirio don't see much of each other — he is so busy with the mines and all. You really haven't had a chance to get to know each other. He's such an extraordinary and brilliant young man. Of course, there are some who think him spoiled. I hate to confess this, lest you think me disloyal, but he *is* spoiled. He was made over as a child, by his sisters. He was always handsome, even in the cradle. Girls spoiled him. His professors at the university spoiled him. I have never blamed Porfirio for what others have done to him. Really, I don't. Beneath all the outward things — the self-assurance that some call arrogance, the single-mindedness that shuts out the world, his vanity, and how vain he is! — beneath all this is a lovable young man. You have found him so, I am sure."

Spoiled, self-centered, vain, handsome? Yes! Brilliant? Possibly. Lovable, no. But how could I say these things to Doña Octavia? Fortunately, I didn't have to. The men and their wives came in at that moment — the Orozcos, Captain Vega and his pretty young wife, the Zoyos — followed by Dr. Beltrán and Villaverde. Porfirio did not appear. Holding me by the hand, Doña Octavia spoke to Villaverde as he came through the door.

At dinner, dressed in one of his Renaissance costumes — puffed sleeves and yards of lace (he had spindly legs, which he filled out with pads and elastic beneath his red silk stockings) — he had been in good spirits. "The Spanish government is seriously thinking of laying claim to Isla del Oro," he said as he spooned his soup. About his role as guardian he said nothing.

"*Señor,*" Doña Octavia now informed him, "aren't you glad that Dr. Beltrán has moved into Castillo Santiago? Isn't it a splendid idea?"

Villaverde shook his head ruefully. "Splendid, except that I'm jealous that Miss Lucinda has never invited me to share a tower."

He smiled and took a pinch of snuff from his little gold box, stuffing it daintly into his nose, first one nostril and then the other. He was trying to be gaily jealous, but I recalled that during dinner, at the moment Dr. Beltrán alluded to his residence in the castle, a shadow had darkened his face.

The shadow was still there, hovering over his thin lips and somber eyes. It was there when I resumed my place at the harpsichord.

I played for an hour, but Porfirio never appeared. I didn't see him again until two days later, and then by chance. I was awakened at dawn by the sound of screaming gulls. During the night a storm had swept in from the Aleutians, and gray waves pounded the shore, sending spume high up the castle walls.

After breakfast, as I was on my way to the tower, I caught a glimpse through a window streaming with rain of a lone man riding along the road that led up from the village. When the figure drew closer and I recognized the horse, then the horseman, I ran to the door that opened on the terrace.

Porfirio rode to the terrace steps and was about to dismount when he saw me standing in the doorway. He hesitated, changed his mind at the sight of me, and slipped back into the saddle.

He wore a cloak but was bareheaded. The rain was drenching his face. He shouted something I didn't hear. At the sound, the stallion reared and bore him away. Using his heavy Spanish spurs, he brought the horse back closer this time, so close that the beast's front hooves rested on the first step of the terrace, not five strides away.

"Why are you sitting there in the rain?" I asked him. "You'll drown."

He took his time answering. His hair, always carefully combed, fell dripping over his forehead.

I left the doorway and its protecting canopy and took a step toward him. Standing in the rain, I said, "Are you angry at me?"

It was a silly question to ask, deserving of silence. He said nothing.

"You are angry about Dr. Beltrán," I said, clumsily repeating myself. "Don't you think it's wise to have him here in the castle in case something happens again? Like the bushmaster thing?"

He brushed the hair from his eyes. "What did the doctor do about the bushmaster? Sit and talk?"

"More than you," I said, though I didn't really mean to say it. "You were asleep, *señor.*"

Porfirio groaned in disgust. He set the heavy spurs against the stallion's flanks and plunged away, heading for the road to the village. Instead he made a wide circle of the driveway and rode back, bringing the stallion to a halt even closer, halfway up the terrace steps.

He brushed the rain from his eyes. Looking down at me, he said, "What did you and the doctor do besides sit and talk? Since he's an Arab, perhaps you got to your knees and both of you faced east, in the direction of Mecca, and prayed, thanking Allah for saving your life. And afterward, did the doctor recite one of his Oriental love poems while he held your lily-white hand?"

"Arabs," I said coolly and pedantically, "are not Orientals. Arabs are people who live in Arabia and adjacent North Africa. Orientals, on the other hand, belong to a geographical division comprising Southern Asia and the Malay Archipelago, as far as and including the Philippines, Borneo, and Java."

Porfirio said quietly, mimicking my pedantic tone, "You've spent sleepless nights racking your little head in a crazy, hopeless search for someone you think is trying to harm you. Did it ever occur to you that the one you're searching for might be this Oriental Arab, Dr. Beltrán?"

"That would only occur to me," I answered, "if I didn't have a head at all — little or big."

"I see . . ."

He choked on the words. I backed away from his blazing eyes. He followed me onto the terrace. Then, fearfully, I turned and fled into the castle. With an oath and a clanking of spurs, he followed me.

I am not certain, but this is what must have taken place in those next few moments. As the stallion leaped through the doorway he must have seen his image there before him in the great Venetian mirror. At that instant, he must have thought that it was an enemy, another stallion charging down upon him, for a horrible cry came from his throat as he reared, then plunged headlong into the mirror.

The sound of shattering glass filled the cavernous

hall. There was no sound from Porfirio. He lay on his side, his face a mass of shards and blood.

The big stallion plunged past us and vanished into the rain.

19.

The Fiery Meteor

PORFIRIO SURVIVED THE ACCIDENT IN THE GREAT Hall of Castillo Santiago. He survived because Dr. Beltrán, at breakfast in the morning room, heard the howling wind, the thunder of shattering glass, the awful screams that followed, and ran to his side.

Porfirio received no broken bones, but a shard of glass, sharper than a knife, cut a curving gash from temple to chin, drawing one corner of his mouth up in an odd way. He would have wished it otherwise — would have preferred shattered bones.

The fear that he was no longer handsome obsessed him. During the first days, when Dr. Beltrán was taking care of him, he never left his rooms and allowed no one in except the doctor, not even his mother and Father Martínez. His meals were left on a tray outside the door. I talked to him every day through the door, but the answers were brief and muffled by his bandages.

Doña Octavia was beside herself with worry. "He was such a handsome young man," she said to me mournfully, her fat fingers plucking at her rings. "I'm sorry he has mirrors in his room. If only he couldn't see himself. I have told him that plastic surgeons in these days can do marvels, but he won't listen, poor boy."

Finally Porfirio let Father Martínez come in. He left with a long face, but after that, before mass in the morning and vespers at dusk, he went each day to visit Porfirio. Neither his mother nor I could coax anything from Father Martínez save curt answers and silence. But in time, though he told us little, I got the impression from Father Martínez that Porfirio had begun to look at life differently.

More than a month went by before Porfirio came out of his rooms. And then it was in the dark, before daybreak, to ride the milk-white stallion. From my tower I saw a spectral figure leave the castle and ride into the hills, morning after morning for weeks.

I believe that he blamed himself for the injuries, for failing as a horseman at a moment of peril and allowing the beast to be his master. Now he would ride until the day, the hour, this was changed and he himself became the master.

Centurion showed no trace of his mad attack upon his image in the mirror. He glistened with lather, his nostrils flared red, and the silver headstall, hawksbells, and bridle shone. He was the same beautiful beast I remembered, but Porfirio had changed. He had changed so much I scarcely recognized him.

A thick black stubble hid his cheeks and chin, except where it parted to show a long livid streak from the cut he had suffered. Nor did it hide the twist at one corner of his mouth. For an instant I thought I was looking at Victor Hugo's hero in *The Man Who Laughed.*

"Yes, I have changed," he said one morning, noticing my surprise. "If you find me repulsive, you are welcome to look the other way."

"I like your beard," I said, and that was how I felt. His smile was disconcerting, because he had seldom smiled, and then as a rule sardonically. It made him seem more human. Yet as he sat there on the big stallion, I concluded that he couldn't have changed that much. Underneath there lurked the Spanish grandee, arrogant, self-centered, and, as his mother seemed proud to proclaim, spoiled. I was a romantic schoolgirl to have believed anything else.

"While I rode this morning," he said, "a thought came to me. I have been forever getting over this accident. Weeks have gone by, months, and the scar seems no better. I think that Beltrán wishes to see me disfigured. He's deliberately handling things to this end."

I was shocked. "Dr. Beltrán saved your life," I reminded him. "You would have bled to death there on the marble floor. No one could have saved you. Neither the servants nor I. No one!"

Porfirio glared at me, angered by my words, still suspicious of Dr. Beltrán. I was standing on the highest step of the terrace, and we were face to face. Never shifting his gaze, he tried to stare me down.

A ghostly hand out of the past seemed to grip me, and I turned away. I had to clench my teeth not to run, not to flee as I had once before. The fear that despite his awful accident he would again pursue me headlong into the castle was all that held me back. But for some reason, from somewhere — was it from pity, from compassion? — the fear faded and disappeared.

"It was Dr. Beltrán who staunched your wounds," I said, surprised at my confident voice. "You would not be here except for his unselfish help. You owe your life to him, Porfirio."

He lowered his gaze, crossed one rein over the other, crossed it back, then looked at me again. This time he didn't try to stare me down. I wanted to think that he was contrite, yet I knew better.

"You wouldn't be here now," I said, "sitting on your fine gold-mounted saddle, clasping a gold saddle horn, attired in fine *vaquero* chaps and jacket, Spanish rowels on the heels of your boots, so dashing and splendid in your new beard — none of this, Porfirio, except for Dr. Beltrán."

I expected him to respond in some way — to object modestly to my compliments, to bow, to laugh. Instead, with the glee of a schoolboy escaping from school, he set spurs to the big stallion, circled the broad driveway twice, and came back, scattering dust, to rear the horse not a stride from where I stood. Reaching down, he then planted a kiss upon my brow.

148

For a moment I was touched by this show of tenderness, an emotion he had never shown me before. And yet, was it really an act of tenderness? Wasn't it, more likely, something else? High spirits? Yes, the same spirits that had prompted him to gallop the stallion around the driveway in an arrogant show of horsemanship.

"I'll be glad to get back at work again," he said. "I went to the smelter this morning and made another survey. Satisfied myself that we can recover without extensive changes most of the gold that's been dumped carelessly into Bahía de Oro. On the way back I stopped at Mine Number One, the Discovery Mine. The elevators are in and the men are working."

"They have been at work for a long time," I said.

Porfirio frowned. "Don't remind me of all the precious weeks I've wasted, sitting up there in the castle. Tomorrow I'll be hard at work on the tunnel. You'll be astounded at the gold that will pour forth. We'll have to do away with the donkey train and purchase trucks. Barges that the *Infanta* can tow. It will be what is called in mining terms a bonanza."

"*Bonanza* comes from words meaning a calm sea, hence good luck," I said, just to say something, appalled at the vision of trucks snorting up and down the hills, the harbor stuffed with shipping, the smelters spewing smoke, Castillo Santiago trembling night and day from the sullen roar of dynamite.

"Calm seas, good luck, whatever the word means," Porfirio said, "it's a fabulous bonanza."

At dinner that night, he retailed the story of the discovery in Mine Number One.

"When I was at the university," he said, "thinking of the day when I would be here on Isla del Oro, I never dreamed that I would discover a spectacular lode of solid gold, a yard wide and at least a mile long."

"Next week I'll celebrate a mass to give thanks for this miracle," Father Martínez said. "But I suggest to you now that you give thought to repairs. You might even consider a new chapel. Yes, a new chapel. With such a rich discovery, you'll need double the number of workers now in the mine. The present chapel is barely adequate."

"A chapel, by all means," Porfirio said, "with a gold altar. And fresh gems for the Madonna. Splendid pearls and diamonds and rubies from the best collections in Spain."

"And a new hospital," Dr. Beltrán said, "with up-to-date equipment. I am hampered now."

"Draw the plans," Porfirio said. "And we'll not forget the latest devices to save lives."

Doña Octavia clasped her hands and raised her eyes toward the ceiling, expressing a wish that I well understood. Doña Catalina gave the matter thought, but finally shook her head and was silent.

Captain Vega asked for an extension to his armory, a dozen white horses of Arabian stock, fifty machine guns, and as many fast-firing magnums for his *pistoleros*. Captain Orozco wanted a more efficient radar, one with a range of two hundred miles. Alicia, who was there waiting on table, collected numerous requests from the servants and presented them in a neat list, which she quietly handed to Porfirio with the salad.

While we made these requests of Porfirio, which were light-hearted but earnest, Señor Villaverde was quiet. Dressed in the black robe and pointed black hood of the Grand Inquisitor, bolt upright in his regal chair, he waited until the last.

"Do not forget," he said to Porfirio, "that it was I who led you to the abandoned tunnel and was so hopeful about the chance of new discoveries."

"Never! I am not one to forget," Porfirio replied. "In your honor, I wish to call the discovery La Galería de Villaverde. Furthermore, I propose a resounding toast to you at this very moment. *Hola* La Galería de Villaverde!"

I couldn't make out Villaverde's face, hidden as it was by the inquisitorial hood, but there was an ominous look to his body, a rigid clasping of his bony hands, that told me he was infuriated at the role Porfirio had suddenly assumed.

As for myself, I was not in the least surprised. At the moment he raced the stallion in front of the terrace, using the big Spanish spurs and a cruel bit, reaching down to favor me with a kiss, I knew that the time Porfirio had spent brooding over his mutilated face hadn't changed him. He was and always would be the man his mother had described at length and so truthfully.

Rising to my feet and lifting my glass of wine, I

said, "And also, my friends, a rousing toast to the memory of Juan Rodriguez Cabrillo, who on this day, nearly five hundred years ago, first sighted the beautiful coast of California."

Of our household, only Salvador Zoyo was not there to make a request. He was in the village with his *penitentes*. During lulls in the conversation, I could hear through the open windows sounds from their reed flutes.

Since the music room was too small for the hundreds of guests invited to come after dinner, we held the celebration in the Great Hall. All of the lamps along the tapestried walls were turned off, and the light came from a thousand candles in the huge chandelier that hung from the ceiling at the center of the room. Below it, the servants had set up my harpsichord on a small platform decorated with flowers.

The night was moonless and clear. The breeze that wandered in from the terrace smelled of the sea. Everyone was in a festive mood, especially the Indian children, so festive that when I sat down to play, Porfirio had to ask for silence.

I had prepared handwritten programs for the occasion — ones with fancy handkerchiefs folded in for the women and children, and initialed ones for the men — featuring the servants' chorus and, immodestly, myself. I played first and was in the middle of "El Rancho Grande," with some of the audience shouting a wild accompaniment, when I was seized by hiccups. Thoughtfully, with scarcely a note missed,

Doña Catalina jumped up and took over the keyboard while I retired.

She was playing the piece, presumably for the second time, for everyone by now had joined in, when I came out of the powder room, clutching a glass of water that I sipped through a handkerchief — a sovereign remedy for this ailment.

As an encore I was supposed to play a rollicking Nayarit melody, but the hiccups, though diminished, were still with me. The duenna again took my place and played the song with a flourish that delighted the children.

I was sitting near the platform, still sipping water through the handkerchief. Doña Catalina had just finished the last bar and was on her feet, spreading her bouffant dress in a pretty bow.

For some reason I thought that the next sound I heard came from the harpsichord, a thin, tinkling echo of the last note she had played. Then there was a louder sound, as of one of the strings breaking or of several breaking at the same time.

I dropped my glass of water. The ceiling seemed to fall. Then it was not the ceiling but the great chandelier and its thousand flaming candles that was falling, slowly, slowly.

Doña Catalina had just finished another bow. The folds of her bouffant skirt had settled at her sides. She was in the act of tossing a kiss to the audience when the great chandelier fell like a fiery meteor.

20.

Covenant

THE ACCIDENT OF DOÑA CATALINA'S DEATH, IF IN-
deed it was an accident, we made no effort to explain.
I went at once to the ship with Porfirio and Captain
Orozco, and there, though I dreaded another invasion
like the one that had taken place after my father's
death, I notified the Los Angeles police. Before I did
so, I had a brief argument with Porfirio.

"Why go to the trouble?" he asked as we stood on
the *Infanta*'s bridge. "We can take care of this without
their help."

In his short time on Isla del Oro, Porfirio, if not so
rabid as Villaverde about the *gringos,* had come to
look upon the mainland as a separate country.

"If Doña Catalina's death is not reported," I said,
"we will be arrested. It is the law."

"On Isla del Oro," Porfirio said, "we, you and I, are
the law."

At my summons the police arrived the next morn-

154

ing, and having told me over the radio not to touch a thing, they spent the first hour dragging the body out from the tangle of candles and steel. At noon *Infanta* set off for the mainland, carrying the corpse of Doña Catalina de Portago.

By afternoon sightseers were arriving in boats of all sizes to cruise up and down the shore with their binoculars trained upon Castillo Santiago. Planes and helicopters flew overhead. My lawyer, Don Anselmo de Alicantera, arrived the next afternoon, bringing with him a copy of the will Villaverde had presented for probate. An hour before he arrived, the two detectives who had come with the police took Porfirio and me to the Great Hall.

We stood around the wrecked chandelier, which was festooned with spires and spears of congealed wax, and answered the detectives' questions. The men were young and apparently competing with each other.

For example, Mr. Carey, a redhead with green eyes, said, "How many in the audience knew that Miss Portago, the deceased, would be playing the harpsichord?"

Before I could answer, Mr. McLaughlin took from his pocket one of the programs I had hand-printed, and said, "No one knew. No one who received one of these. And I assume everyone did. According to the program, Miss Benivides was the only artist scheduled to play the harpsichord."

Mr. McLaughlin, who had long sideburns that hid his ears and a small curtain of blond hair combed halfway down his forehead, said, "Why then was Miss Portago playing?"

"I had a fit of hiccups, and she took my place," I said.

Mr. McLaughlin coughed. Then Mr. Carey asked me how the candles in the chandelier were lit. "There are hundreds. It must be quite a chore," he said.

"What would Miss Benivides know about candles?" Mr. McLaughlin said. "She has dozens of servants who attend to such menial chores."

The questions of who lit the candles, and were they lit from a ladder or from the floor, and were they lit every night or only on special occasions, and was the chandelier a part of the castle when it was built or a fixture which was added later, led in time to the servants, two stout Indian girls, who among their other duties attended to the chandelier. They directed us to a ladder ascending from an alcove at one end of the Great Hall, where cleaning utensils were stored, to a narrow crawlway.

The crawlway opened into a large loft. In this space stood a windlass and a gear box, the machinery by which the big chandelier was lowered for the thousand candles to be lit, then drawn up and locked into position so that it flooded the Great Hall with light.

Cobwebs hung from the loft ceiling, and a carpet of ancient dust covered the floor, except for a path worn from the ladder to the windlass by bare Indian feet. On both sides of the path lay discarded objects, also covered with dust.

I was embarrassed as Mr. Carey's torch played over this scene. "I'll have the girls clean up this mess tomorrow," I said.

"Don't touch it," he said. "We may find a clue somewhere in the debris."

Mr. McLaughlin examined the windlass. "The wire that held the chandelier was cut."

"Which means that it was not an accident," Mr. Carey said.

"Murder," Mr. McLaughlin said. "And whoever it was might possibly, just possibly, have tried to murder you, not Miss Portago. Have there been other attempts on your life?"

I told him about the accidents at Bahía de Oro, at the mine, and my experience with the bushmaster — some but not all of the things that had happened.

He shook his head. "You should have reported them before. We might have saved a life."

"Or tried to," Mr. Carey added.

Downstairs, as we stood on the terrace in the bright sunshine, he asked about Superintendent Zoyo.

"Zoyo is in charge of the mines. Where was he at the hour the flood at the smelter was let loose?"

"In the village," Porfirio answered. "At least that is what he told me."

"But he could have been there in the smelter when you first asked for him, an hour before the flood," Mr. McLaughlin said. "Where was he later when the steps broke and the miner was killed?"

"In the mine," Porfirio said. "And he was there when I was nearly trapped."

A rubberneck ship went by, close on shore, so near that I could hear voices and distinguish people clutching cameras, lined up along the rail. Mr. McLaughlin said, "Is there any reason why Zoyo should want to do away with you?"

"A very good reason," Porfirio said. "He's afraid of me. I have criticized the way he's running the mines. His old-fashioned methods that waste millions. Zoyo's afraid I'll fire him."

He started to explain what he meant by "old-fashioned," but Mr. McLaughlin said, "Am I to understand that you're engaged to marry Miss Benivides?" Before Porfirio could answer, he asked, "How long have you been engaged?"

"For years," Porfirio said, bristling at what he took to be a suspicious, prying question.

"For years?" repeated Mr. Carey. "But Miss Benivides is only seventeen."

"The engagement was arranged by our parents. It's a Spanish custom, a custom of the nobility."

"Long engagements are common in our country," I said for no reason at all, except that I was terribly disturbed.

Mr. Carey, brushing down the fringe of hair on his forehead that the sea breeze was playing with, said, "Dr. Beltrán. I have talked to the doctor and found him an interesting gentleman. A foreigner, isn't he?"

"An Arab," Porfirio promptly replied.

"I see," Mr. Carey said, as if he did "see" something.

"Arab, scarab, what difference does it make what

he is?" Mr. McLaughlin wanted to know.

"None," I said, and received a hard stare from Porfirio.

The rubberneck steamer was coming back, cruising closer to shore this time. Passengers were pointing at the castle, their cameras flashing in the sun.

"Captain Vega we haven't talked to yet," Mr. Carey said. He's out with his men patrolling the island, we were informed."

I believe that the detective thought of Captain Vega as a prime suspect.

At this moment Señor Villaverde appeared on the terrace. He had a basket of bread in his hand and was feeding a flock of gulls hovering above him. He would take a few steps, tear off a piece of bread and toss it into the air, and then move on along the terrace.

"Mr. Villaverde we haven't talked to either," Mr. Carey said. "I understand he's your guardian."

"Not yet," I said. "My father's will hasn't been probated."

"But you will be his ward?"

"Most likely."

Villaverde came up and greeted us with a courtly bow, the gulls still hovering above his head. He was dressed in the costume of an eighteenth-century matador — short trousers with ribbons at the knee, a tight, black, embroidered jacket, and a black handkerchief binding his hair — like the matadors you see in the elegant etchings of Francisco Goya.

"I feel left out," he said, smiling his most engaging smile, the one in which he showed all of his teeth.

"You have talked to maids, butlers, stableboys, coachmen, gardeners, to Zoyo, to Dr. Beltrán, to Captain Orozco, to everyone except me and Captain Vega. He only because he is out patrolling the island, protecting it from a ravaging horde."

He paused a moment to tear off pieces of bread and toss them to the screaming gulls.

"Since I am soon to be the guardian of Señorita Lucinda de Cabrillo y Benivides," he went on, "my sole thought and concern is to relieve her of the distress she plainly feels — how pale she looks — in connection with the death of Doña Catalina. To that end, I suggest that she be permitted to leave us and repair to her tower."

Taken aback by his flow of words, no less than by his costume and the flock of gulls, the detectives gazed at him for a while, then Mr. McLaughlin said that I was at liberty to leave at any time I wished.

Villaverde paused again to feed the gulls that wove back and forth. One that looked exactly like the rest — gray wings, white body, and yellow beak — was his favorite. As he held out the bread, it settled down and ate from his hand. Was I mistaken? Did I hear him correctly? Did he call the bird Lucinda?

While this was going on, Mercedes came to say that Don Anselmo was waiting for me in the library.

"Just you, Lucinda," she said when Señor Villaverde started to follow us into the castle. Silently, he followed us anyway, as did the two detectives.

The four of us sat down around my father's big desk with Don Anselmo. I had visited the library only

160

once since the day, months before, when I had seen the shape of his body in the chair, and his cigar in the ashtray — or thought I had. That day seemed to belong to another life.

Don Anselmo gave me a copy of my father's will, since he could not read it himself. It was written as usual in Don Enrique's spidery hand, where all the *l*'s and *t*'s looked much alike and the *q*'s and *g*'s, and *s*'s and *f*'s looked exactly alike, and each line was written from right to left, upside down, so that it could only be read in a mirror.

Don Anselmo said to the detectives, "This was not meant to be a conference, but since you appear interested, kindly remain."

"At this moment," Mr. Carey said, "everything on the island interests me and my partner, Mr. McLaughlin, so we accept your invitation."

Don Anselmo glanced at Señor Villaverde but said nothing. Villaverde was silent.

Mercedes brought a mirror and held it for me. I read slowly, though the script was familiar, translating each word to myself before I said it aloud. My voice was shaky. There were some sentences I didn't translate. I said so and went on.

It was very quiet. My voice echoed in the vast room. There was the distant sound of the surf running along the beach. At one time the mirror shuddered, as a charge of dynamite went off in the tunnel beneath the castle. In one place, where my father had listed among his holdings oil fields in Venezuela, a copper mine in Peru, and thirty miles of the Mexican coast, planted to pineapples and described as the Blue Beach, Mr. McLaughlin asked me to please read the part a second time.

Señor Villaverde sat beside me, his ringed hands folded calmly in his lap. I was unable to see his face, but I did feel his presence and smell the cologne he wore. He sat calmly because he knew the will, word by word. At one place, for instance, when I made a small mistake, he was quick to correct me. Later on, as I read the part that made me his ward, he murmured under his breath, "A grave responsibility."

At last, as I came to the end, there was a long sentence written not in the spidery script of the rest of the will, but in a firmer hand, as if it were meant to be a clear and final word spoken to me across the abyss, a cautionary cry from the grave.

"And be it known," I read, "in the event of my daughter's death, God forbid, that all of my properties, both tangible and intangible, I do bequeath to the companion of my boyhood, the loyal friend of my later years, Don Ricardo Villaverde of Isla del Oro, formerly of Seville, beautiful city of Spain, the mother of us all."

There was a moment of deep silence. The detectives were now writing, Mr. McLaughlin with a pencil, Mr. Carey with a ballpoint pen. I distinguished one sound from the other. Leaning on the desk, Villaverde sat with his chin resting on his clasped hands, a fleeting smile on his lips.

Don Anselmo broke the silence. "This will, as you

know, Lucinda, has not been ruled upon by the court. Meanwhile, acting as your counsel, I've filed suit to have the will declared invalid upon the grounds that your father was of unsound mind on the day he wrote it."

Villaverde at once sat erect. The smile left his face.

"And there is no question that he was of unsound mind," Don Anselmo said. "It has been proven and documented in detail. It can be found in the police file, in the coroner's report."

Villaverde rose to his feet. He cleared his throat to say something and stopped. I believe it was now, at this moment, that he saw the awful truth of Don Anselmo's words — that in the end the courts would surely rule against him.

Silently, he picked up his basket, went to the window, and tossed the last of the bread to the hovering gulls. His favorite gull, the one he had called Lucinda, came and perched on his shoulder. With one quick movement he reached out and wrung its neck.

He came back to the desk but did not take his seat. He stood in his matador costume, head held high and feet firmly planted, as if he were about to face a charging bull.

"*Señor,*" he said to Don Anselmo, "I declare as a humble servant of a just God that He in His majesty will not sit blindly by and idly watch while Isla del Oro, splendid outpost of ancient Spain, is torn asunder. While the hopes and dreams of Don Enrique de Cabrillo y Benivides are desecrated."

He glanced around the desk, at each of us in turn. "No," he warned us all, "God in His might sees and remembers."

Disdaining an answer, with the sly tread of a matador he left the room. The two detectives, overcome by his rhetoric and manner, did nothing to detain him.

21.

One Black Thread

DON ANSELMO AND I WENT BACK TO THE GREAT
Hall, accompanied by the detectives. The chandelier
remained in a tangled heap where it had fallen. A
shred of Doña Catalina's bouffant dress still clung to
one of the candles.

Mr. Carey, looking at his notebook, said, "While
you were in the audience, Miss Benivides, before you
sat down to play, and afterwards while you were at
the harpsichord, or later, did you during any of this
time catch sight of Mr. Villaverde?"

I was about to shake my head when the dimmest of
memories took hold of me. "Yes, I do remember
something. A man standing alone against the wall. He
was not far from me as I sat down at the harpsichord."

Then the memory faded.

"Think," Mr. McLaughlin prompted me.

Mr. Carey said, "Was the man you saw standing
against the wall dressed in black?"

"It's possible," I said.

"Think hard," Mr. McLaughlin said. "It's important."

"Was he or wasn't he dressed in black?" Mr. Carey asked.

"In black," I answered, though I wasn't sure.

Mr. McLaughlin glanced at his notebook. "Does Mr. Villaverde have a habit of dressing up in various costumes? Today he was a Spanish something-or-other."

"A matador," Mr. Carey said. "A Spanish or Mexican matador."

"Can you remember what Mr. Villaverde wore on the night of the recital?" Mr. McLaughlin asked.

I remembered clearly. "At dinner that night, before the recital, he was dressed in the garb of the Grand Inquisitor."

"Grand Inquisitor?" Mr. Carey said doubtfully.

"The man who headed the Spanish Inquisition," I explained, "which started in the year fourteen-eighty and lasted until the year eighteen forty-three, was called the Grand Inquisitor. He examined heretics and consigned them to the flames. There were many inquisitors . . ."

Mr. Carey interrupted me. "The Grand Inquisitor wore black?"

"Yes, somber black."

"Was the man you saw standing against the wall that night dressed in somber black?" Mr. Carey asked.

Suddenly I remembered that I hadn't seen the

166

man's face. I hadn't seen it because he was wearing a hood.

Mr. McLaughlin took a folded paper from his pocket. Inside was a length of coarse, black thread, which he held to the light.

"Would this thread," he asked, "be approximately the color of the costume Mr. Villaverde wore that night at dinner?"

"To my knowledge it's the same," I said, turning it over in my hand.

"We found the thread in the loft, snagged on the arm of the windlass, probably when the machine was turning."

"We searched Villaverde's quarters and found the costume it came from," Mr. Carey said.

Porfirio strode in at this point, frowning because he had neither been invited to hear the will read nor included in the present meeting.

"What have you found?" he said to the detectives. "Anything at all? Have you talked to Salvador Zoyo? To Dr. Beltrán? A leading suspect, as I see it."

Mr. McLaughlin put away the thread, and both men made notes.

My heart beat so hard I couldn't speak. The thought that Villaverde had quietly left the hall, climbed the stairs, and made his way to the loft, had gone there secretly when he knew that I was at the harpsichord, and by groping in the dark had deliberately unloosed the chandelier — this was beyond belief. Then, as I recalled the last sentence of the will, where my father had written that upon my death the island became the property of Ricardo Villaverde, a different light was shed upon this act, upon the other attempts to kill me.

"You're pale," Porfirio said. "Come and we'll sit somewhere, and then I'll return and talk to these kind gentlemen. I am sure you'll understand," he said to the detectives.

We left the Great Hall and went to the terrace and down the winding stairs to the belvedere that hung like an eagle's nest above the sea. Of rare woods from the Orient and roofed with gold plates, it had been my father's favorite place to spend late afternoons, before the mainland lights came on, and dream of the past, the days when Cabrillo first sighted the island and the years when Father Serra built his missions along the California coast.

To suit my mood, the sky that afternoon should have been an ominous gray with driving clouds, and the sea a maelstrom of furious waves. Instead, the sky was clear. A pearly sheen covered the west and the setting sun. The tide was ebbing among the rocks without the smallest sound.

Porfirio was very handsome with his new, carefully trimmed beard, his face glowing in the last of the sun.

"This business about who murdered the duenna will go on and on," he said. "The detectives will prowl for days. Perhaps weeks, who knows? Castillo Santiago is a comfortable place to prowl." He put his hand on mine. "It's a terrible ordeal. Far too much to ask of one little girl. From now on I'll take charge of the mess. I'll get the authorities off the island, *muy pronto*. You should have called upon me long before this. Next time remember that Porfirio . . ."

I took my hand away, as gently as I could, struck suddenly by a voice from the past. My whole life had been lived under the iron fist of my father, who at times had loved me and at times had hated me, who always knew what should please me the most, what I should and should not do.

The sun had disappeared. A pink glow was spreading over the sea and the beach and the rocks the belvedere rested upon, upon Porfirio himself.

I said to him, "My father arranged for me to marry you. Your father and mother arranged for you to marry me. Neither one of us had anything to do with the arrangement. Now here we are, engaged to be married, but neither of us in love. We are friends, that's all. Good friends, I believe and hope."

"That's enough, dear Lucinda," Porfirio said, taking my hand again.

His words hung in the air. He glanced up at the gulls above the belvedere. They were drifting in the windless sky, ready to fly homeward for the night.

He laughed. "You can't expect people to fall in love at first sight," he said. "In a few short months."

His tone was charming, confident. He was certain that all we needed was a little time on the island together and then love could come stealing upon us, magically out of a scented night. He was mistaken. It never would.

Gently, as gently as I could, I took my hand away for the last time and forever.

A series of small blasts shook the belvedere.

"We'll have some real blasts when we start working the new vein," Porfirio said.

22.

The Quetzal

AFTERWARD, WHEN WE WENT IN TO DINNER, SEÑOR
Villaverde was not present. Father Martínez had
talked to him at early mass. At dusk Mercedes had
seen him in the village and then on the wharf, but he
had not boarded the ship, Captain Orozco said.
Obeying police orders, Vega had stationed *pistoleros*
at strategic places around the island. "He has not
escaped us," said the captain, who had always feared
Villaverde. "Nor will he."

Dinner was an hour of gloom. There was little talk,
except by Porfirio, who explained to Don Anselmo
what he was doing at Mine Number One and the detail of what he planned for Bahía de Oro. Doña Octavia, who had not come out of her rooms since the
night of the murder, was quiet and didn't enjoy her
food. The servants slipped back and forth like so
many specters.

I went to bed early but didn't sleep. There were

small sounds from the castle, servants moving about on the stairs, and in the village, songs and the strumming of guitars. I heard a squad of Captain Vega's *pistoleros* ride along the beach on their nightly patrol. *Infanta*'s big marine clock struck the hour, six bright notes that floated upward on the warm air. At first I thought they were the chirpings of the quetzal.

I got out of bed and went to its cage. I found the bird fast asleep. I opened the cage, took it out, and held it against my breast until it awakened. Then I went to the window.

For a brief moment I stood there with the beautiful bird in my arms, doubting the wisdom of what I was about to do. The quetzal was far from home. Could it cross the channel and find its way south into the hot lands? But birds migrated, flew for thousands of miles, far beyond Central America, to Peru and beyond. Even the delicate hummingbird migrated, by the thousands. It was night, but there was a full moon, and the quetzal was a bird of the night.

I placed it on the window ledge. In case it wanted to return to its cage, I left the window open. I went back to bed, and again I didn't sleep. Toward dawn, before the first light appeared in the east, the bird tried its wings. They hadn't been used in months, but without a sound, it rose in the air. There was a flash of yellow and green and scarlet, and the quetzal, the most beautiful bird of all the birds in the world, was gone.

I dozed and awakened — it could not have been more than a few minutes later, for it was still dark — to the sound of a heavy explosion. For an instant I

172

thought that it had happened in my dreams. But I was no longer in bed. I lay on the floor, gasping for breath.

I was accustomed to explosions — they took place every day. Sometimes there was a series of them as blasting went on in the different mines, especially in Mine Number One, whose galleries traveled in expanding circles beneath the castle. But I had never been thrown out of bed before.

I got to my feet and ran to the window. The moon was down in the west, but by its waning light I saw people far below in the village street running from their huts. In the harbor, *Infanta*'s big searchlight suddenly swept the sky.

Two days earlier an earthquake had rocked the mainland and we had felt its tremors and the aftershocks. This could be another earthquake — they seemed to occur in cycles. *Infanta*'s searchlight swung slowly through the sky, hesitated for an instant, then fastened itself on the castle and remained there, like a warning eye.

The light was blinding. I turned away and went to the door. The passageway was deserted. I waited, expecting another blast. It came at once, less violent than the first, and as nearly as I could tell, not from the mine but from deep in the castle.

I hurried into a jumper, wound my hair, and shoved it under a cap. Candles guttered in the corridor, reeking smoke as they died. No sounds came from below, but far off in the village dogs had begun to bark.

I took the main stairs, where night lights were still burning, and went to the Great Hall. Mercedes stood at the entrance, clutching her pink wrapper. The door was half open, and she peered out into the gray dawn. A carriage was moving up the road from the village. I heard the driver shout and crack his whip.

"It's Doctor Beltrán," Mercedes said. "There was an accident last night at the wharf. He's coming back."

"The explosions?" I said.

"Below somewhere."

"In the mine?"

"I guess. That's where they usually are."

"They woke me up."

"I was already awake," Mercedes said.

I noticed now, as she turned toward me, that her face was strained. "What's wrong?" I asked her. "You're not frightened?"

"Not at the explosion. I've gotten used to explosions over the years. There was one when you were two years old that shook the roof off a tower."

The carriage ground to a halt in the driveway and Dr. Beltrán jumped out. He rushed past as if he hadn't seen us, then turned and ran back.

"The madman's loose," he said and then said it again. There was blood on his shirt from a cut somewhere. "Have you seen Villaverde?"

Mercedes said, "I was asleep. It was after midnight, about one. A knock on my door woke me up. It was Villaverde. He wanted the key to the closet that's on my floor. I told him he couldn't have the key and to

174

go away, which he did after some wild groans."

"It must have been later that he came to the hospital," Dr. Beltrán said. "I was in the operating room. An emergency. He burst in on me and demanded pills. I had a tussle with him but gave him a handful and he left. He was riding a horse, and I heard him galloping up the hill toward the chapel. After that, an hour or more afterward, I heard a loud explosion. Then a second one. I finished with my patient and I'm here. Have you seen him?"

Dr. Beltrán's words were lost in a blast that shook the marble floor. The sound came from the direction of the passageway that connected the crypt to the tunnel that led to the mine.

23.

"My Name Is
Ozymandias"

DAWN WAS BREAKING. THE WHOLE CASTLE—
servants and guests, Don Anselmo, Doña Octavia, everyone except Porfirio — had gathered in the Great
Hall. They were huddled in a quiet group, waiting for
someone to tell them what to do.

Father Martínez herded them outside to the terrace.
He decided to take them to the chapel, but another
blast changed his mind and he took them away from
the castle, down the long *portale* to a garden surrounded by a high stone fence. As I stood on the terrace, frightened, utterly confused, Porfirio and Dr.
Beltrán came up.

At that moment another blast rocked the terrace.
The sound came from the direction of Mine Number
One. Seized by a sudden thought, I led the two men to
the stairway that wound beneath the castle to the pantheon and crypt.

Votive candles were alight in the pantheon, casting an eerie glow on the tombs of Juan Cabrillo and Gaspar de Portolá and my father. The flowers that bedecked the tombs must have been placed there within the hour, possibly by Villaverde, for they were fresh and sparkled with dew.

I had an intense feeling that he was somewhere near, perhaps in the crypt we were approaching. Perhaps on the tortuous stairs that wound upward from it to my tower, the ones I once thought the serpent had taken on its nocturnal journey. Perhaps in the mine.

Since I was acquainted with the passages, I took the lead and listened at the gold-banded door before I opened it. A strong odor of incense assailed me. Light from the candles blazed on the marble walls and the crystal caskets. The candles had been lit only moments before, the wicks scarcely burned.

I went past the row of crystal caskets and, on an impulse, to the door that opened into the mine. Here, having collected a pair of candles, Porfirio insisted upon taking the lead.

There was a bitter smell of burned powder. Wisps of smoke stung my eyes. At a narrow place in the passage where we rounded an abrupt turn, I saw eyes gleaming in the dark, not ten strides away, small and fiery red — the eyes of my father's staghounds.

Villaverde stood beside the hounds, leaning against the wet stones of the tunnel. His legs were crossed as though he were standing on some quiet corner in a pleasant town, but in his hand he held a large pistol.

"Buenos días," he said without surprise, as though he were expecting us, but in a strained and unfriendly voice.

Stunned, no one returned his greeting.

"I would invite you to sit down," he said, "if there were chairs. I would give you tea, were there tea and servants to serve it."

Beyond him a stride or so, candles burned on a stone shelf. Behind the shelf was a small alcove filled with waxed packages marked $T + T + T$, figures used to label explosives of triple strength.

"Lacking all three, chairs and tea and servants, I must ask your pardon," Señor Villaverde said, "and simply bid you welcome."

The pistol he was pointing at us was ancient but deadly. I recognized it as an antique of my father's with two enormous barrels, one below the other; my father had prized it because it had killed many Moors in the battle for Granada.

"Truthfully, my friends," Villaverde said, "I also lack the time for anything more than the briefest of chats."

He waved the antique gun in the direction of the alcove. I hadn't noticed it before, but peering into the darkness I made out a length of white cord leading out of the alcove and running along the floor in a series of loops to where Villaverde stood.

"Porfirio," he said, "since you are a mining engineer, or at least have ambitions to become one, it may interest you to know that the fuse I am about to light is of the best quality — not common acid, but acid

178

made of mercury salts." He bent down and calmly touched the candle flame to the fuse. "I advise you, therefore, to leave without delay, for it is prompt and certain, as soon as I have spoken."

Porfirio was stepping forward to put his foot on the burning cord when Villaverde drew back the hammers on his gun. The two small sounds were no louder than the sputtering of the fuse on the floor.

"You, Porfirio, are an intruder," Villaverde said, pointing the gun. "I knew you would be, and that is why I set assassins on you in the city of Seville. The idiots failed. So you came armed with smart ideas, which have visited a plague upon the island, which threaten it with ruin, which have brought me to this."

He turned to Dr. Beltrán, keeping his gun pointed all the while at Porfirio. "You, sir, are a good man. You came, lured hither by promises I made and could not keep. I am sorry that I will never live to know you better, for in your veins courses the rare and elegant genius of the ancient Moors."

The fuse burned by fits and starts, giving off tiny orange sparks so slowly that it well might burn for an hour.

"To you, Lucinda de Cabrillo y Benivides," he said, "spoiled child and traitoress, I confess that I tried to unseat your reason. Then I tried to end your days on this earth. And I would have done so, except that I foresaw in a moment of blinding revelation that it was better for you to live out your days, to have ample time to suffer for your sins."

He stooped and pinched off the burning fuse, shortening it by half and lighting it again with his big candle. "Leave, all of you," he said.

He aimed at us once more, cocking the two-barreled pistol to its second notch. It made two small sounds, louder now than the fuse sputtering away in the alcove.

"Go," he said. "I am weary with talk."

There was a final, menacing ring to his words that could not be mistaken. Our lives were in danger. Silently, we turned away and retraced our steps down the long corridor, moving as rapidly as we could in the half-darkness.

At the heavy door at the end of the tunnel, Porfirio stepped aside for us to pass. When I didn't move as quickly as he wished, he gave me a shove. "Run!" he said. "Warn Father Martínez!"

We had gone halfway along the row of caskets before I realized that Porfirio was not with us. I glanced back but did not see him. The door into the tunnel was closed. As I left the crypt I glanced back again, looking for him. Awkwardly I slipped on the marble floor and lay sprawled out for a while. Then I heard Dr. Beltrán shout something and his footsteps on the stairway.

I climbed the first flight of stairs and the second. Castillo Santiago loomed above me. The flags of Spain, which Villaverde had never taken down since the day he raised them, hung limp in the windless dawn.

Father Martínez stood at the door of the chapel, surrounded by his silent crowd. In their midst was Dr.

180

Beltrán. I ran toward them, too terrified to make a sound, but before I had taken a dozen steps Doña Octavia stopped me.

"Porfirio!" she cried, clutching my arm. "Where is my son? I've heard a terrible story."

I tried to find my voice. Her fingers bit into my arm, and for a moment I thought she meant to shake the answer out of me.

"Where?" she gasped.

I knew where Porfirio was. He had gone back to talk to Villaverde, to reason with him, to try to persuade him not to set off the cache of TNT — enough powder to move a mountain. And if that failed, if everything failed, to kill the man or be killed himself. I knew all this, yet what could I say to her?

"Where?" she cried, brushing the streaming hair from her eyes. "I heard from Mercedes just now. As we fled from the castle, she told me that my son had gone to find Villaverde. He was with you and the doctor. Where is he now?"

Her grip on my arm tightened. We stared at each other. Her eyes blazed with anger, trying to wring the truth from me.

"Where?" she demanded at the peak of her voice. "Where?"

Dr. Beltrán heard her outcry and came over to where we were standing. He told her calmly that Porfirio was still in the mine.

"You two left him there alone? With the murderer? With Villaverde?"

"We didn't abandon him," I said. "We didn't know

anything until the door closed and he was gone. It was his choice, not ours."

She grew rigid. Blood drained from her face. Then a change came over her slowly. "There was no choice for him," she said. "What would you have a Spaniard do? Would you have him flee? Hide in the castle under his mother's skirts?"

She was right. There had been no choice for Porfirio. Bravery was expected, demanded of him.

"He acted with courage," I said, feeling my heart go out to both of them, mother and son. "He is a brave man," I said. "A very brave man."

Tears came to her eyes. I threw my arms around her, and as I did so, a clatter of hooves sounded on the terrace above us, followed by shouts from Captain Vega. He came hurrying along the porch with a squad of *pistoleros* and, led by Dr. Beltrán, disappeared down the stairway.

Father Martínez motioned for us to follow him into the garden. Doña Octavia, after pausing to catch her breath, went with him and his flock. I heard the gate groan shut behind them and their voices rise in prayer.

I started toward the stairway. Halfway along the porch, I heard a series of muffled sounds. Were they blows delivered by Vega's pistol men — they carried heavy crowbars — in their efforts to batter down the door into the tunnel? Or were they gunshots, the sound of a struggle between Porfirio and Villaverde?

Realizing that gunfire couldn't be heard unless the

door into the tunnel were broken down, I ran ahead, determined to learn what was taking place. I had not gone far when the stones shifted beneath my feet. I ran toward the garden, where Father Martínez and his flock were hidden.

All at once it was quiet. Then the blast came — too loud for the ears, too loud to hear. Around me the air seemed to be gathered up and sucked into the sky. For a while there was no air to breathe.

The south tower moved first, leaning out against the pearly sky like a huge bird about to take wing. Then silently and slowly it toppled to earth. The other towers followed. Then the stones gave way, and floor after floor, the castle crumpled in upon itself.

Quickly, out of the tumbling stones, rose an enormous cloud, hiding the sun and showering the headland with dust. Seabirds flew through the cloud like gray arrows, screaming. Then the waiting sea rushed forward and filled the place where Castillo Santiago had stood. Choosing two paths, one on each side of the crumpled castle, it filled the honeycomb of tunnels and then swept upward against the highest ramparts, as if it meant to engulf the island.

Waves rose to the level of the sea and slowly fell back. The yellow waters grew calm and changed color. A blue tide moved along the new shores, which looked as though they had been there since ancient times.

It was quiet for a while. No sounds came up from below, from the castle that was now beneath the sea.

Above, in the dusty air, the seabirds were also silent. Into my thoughts came words from Shelley's antique traveler:

> *... Two vast and trunkless legs of stone*
> *Stand in the desert ... Near them, on the sand,*
> *Half sunk, a shattered visage lies ...*
> *And on the pedestal these words appear:*
> *"My name is Ozymandias, king of kings:*
> *Look on my works, ye Mighty, and despair!"*

Objects came up out of the deep and began to float about with the tide. On the farthest shore, I saw a black pennon of Spain fastened to its broken pole. Below me, amidst the drifting wreckage, safe in its golden frame, I made out the portrait of Teresa de Benivides. I could not see the smile on her parted lips, yet the message that had meant so much to me in the past was surely there.

Slowly, the garden gate creaked open. Father Martínez peered out at the vacant sea where once my father's castle, built with pride, in defiance and hatred, had stood. Shading his eyes, he held his crucifix up to the bright, cloudless day, high over his head to the rising sun.